Transfiguration

Matt Garrow

For Brian Conroy,
who taught me to write.

Special thanks are due to Justin, whose constant
enthusiasm helped drive this story to completion.

Transfiguration

I

He had punched another hole in his belt because it wasn't tight enough anymore. His arms were bruised from constant scratching. His skin was pale and slick with greasy sweat. His legs never stopped moving. He kept kicking the back of the car seats.

Alden glanced in the rear view mirror. "Calm down," he said. "We're almost there."

In the passenger seat, Doug twisted around and looked past the headrest at his friend. "Look at me, Mark."

The thin man blinked hard and a tear ran down his cheek. His eyes jumped from the floor to Doug and back again.

"Look at me. You sure about this? You don't have to do this, you know. You could give it a few days. Sleep on it."

"No, I have to talk to him," Mark said. His head was shaking fast.

Alden glanced in the mirror again and said plainly, "No, you don't."

"Yes, I do."

"She's just a bitch," Doug said. "That's all. Let it go. Let it go and leave them alone. It's a good reason to get away from all of this anyway, right?" He watched his friend shiver. "Right?"

Alden brought the sedan around a corner. Ahead of him the houses were depressed. Peeling paint. Chipped concrete stoops. Sagging porches of rotting wood. Ripped furniture on lawns of half-dead grass baking in the orange-gold light of the setting summer sun. He slowed the car and shook his head. "You're in no condition to get into a fight."

"I just want to talk to him. We're friends."

"You're a buyer. You're income."

"I just want to talk to him. Just to know about her, for s-sure, you know? I j-just need to know. I just need to ask him. It's cool. I'm okay. Relax."

"You're telling me to relax?"

Alden brought the car to the curb and parked beside a small house one door from the corner. He watched Mark in the mirror as he stared through the window.

"Just want to talk to him."

Alden shifted in his seat and looked at Doug, who looked back with a frown. Alden raised his eyebrows. *What do you want me to do?*

Doug shook his head and turned around. "I'll go with you if you want."

Mark opened his door. "No, it's cool. I'll call you, you know, when I'm ready to go."

"We can wait," Alden offered with a disapproving look to Doug.

"No, go. It's cool, really. It's cool. I'll call you."

Mark shut the door and walked slowly up the cracked concrete walkway, then stumbled on the sun-dried steps to the porch. He knocked on the door and it opened, but Alden couldn't see who was inside.

"You want to wait?" Doug asked.

"What's the use?"

Alden put the car in gear and pulled away from the curb, then turned at the next cross street. It was only a few minutes to downtown, where the derelict suburbs gave way to antique buildings of weathered brick and newer constructions of stone and glass. It was as if he could blink his eyes and transform a sagging porch into a four-story parking garage. The city was built on a hill that sloped toward the large lake to the west, now preparing to touch the falling sun. Only a few buildings were tall enough to interrupt the view. Most of them stood in rows that contained the small shops and restaurants that captured tourists. A few of the newer projects had been built away from the rest; it had caused serious derision between those for aesthetics and those for commerce. Alden brought the car to a long, cobbled street given over to pedestrians and stopped at a stop sign.

"You want to get a bite?" Doug asked.

"Sure."

They crossed the intersection when it was free of shoppers. Alden drove slowly and looked through the side window at the church from which the street took its name. The white steeple was glowing in the rich gold sunlight. He looked forward again and turned a corner. A few blocks away he found a parking space on the side of Main Street. It was a Saturday, but traffic was light. Most people had already eaten dinner and it was too early for the bars to be busy.

"Mark's in trouble," Doug said as they left the car.

Alden shoved his hands into his pockets. "I know."

"I don't get it."

Alden shrugged. At the far end of the street, at the bottom of the long hill, the orange sun was low over the lake. The Adirondacks were a faint purple-gray line, irregular and hazy, on the other side of the water. He took a deep breath of the warm summer air.

They walked up the hill and past a small park behind City Hall a wide brick building with a white clock tower jutting from its pitched roof. A block ahead was a restaurant's rotating neon sign. Its glow was nearly the same color as the sun. The door was open beneath it. At the counter, Alden ordered an open-faced turkey sandwich and Doug said he'd have the same. They waited silently for the cook to make their orders. The old wood paneling here was dark—like it had soaked in the city over the years—and the worn tables and booths felt homey. The other side of the building was a bar and Alden could hear someone tuning a guitar. When the food was ready, Doug asked for extra gravy and they paid and sat in a booth at the back of the room.

"You working tonight?" Alden asked.

"Yeah. Inventory's coming up soon. We're organizing."

"Sounds thrilling."

Doug rolled his eyes. "Ever hear back from that book shop?"

"They never called me back. Seems to happen when they find out you were kicked loose from your last job for breaking policy."

"I told you not to tell them that."

"They'd find out when they checked my reference."

"Really? My company can't tell people anything. They just give them your dates of employment and what you did for work. The department can say what happened?"

"I don't know."

"Bullshit anyway," Doug said. He stabbed at a fry with his fork and wedged it into his mouth. "Like it was a big deal."

"Apparently it was."

"Bullshit. They fuckin' give you a gun, right? You passed all their tests or whatever. What's it matter if you have another one?"

Alden cocked his head slightly in consideration. "Liability issues. They can control your sidearm, document your qualifications and all that. They can't control a backup and they don't want to be liable for something they can't control."

"You should be more pissed."

"I should be thankful the guy didn't have any family to sue me into a homeless shelter."

"*Also* bullshit."

Alden waved his hand. Doug was becoming more animated and he didn't want to talk about this now.

Doug shrugged. "You think Andrea's really fucking that asshole?"

"Maybe."

"I always knew she was a bitch."

Alden nodded slowly. "Maybe Mark will realize that after this guy kicks his ass today."

"We should've stayed there."

"You shouldn't have ordered extra gravy."

Doug shook his head. "Diets are for losers."

Alden chuckled and his cell phone rang. He took it from its plastic holder and flipped it open.

"Hey, Mark," he answered. "Things go alright?"

"Yeah, Tom's giving me a ride home."

"You sure? We're just downtown."

"No, it's cool. I'll call you later."

"Okay." He hung up.

"So?" Doug asked.

"It went well, apparently." Alden held up his hands. "Maybe Andrea didn't leave him for that guy."

"Yeah, well, she's still a bitch."

Doug had the following night off and met Alden at a bar away from the city, beside a strip mall just off the main road. They both considered it a dive, but it was the end of the weekend and it was quieter than downtown. Most of the revelry, if there was any, usually stayed outside on the attached deck. The inside was dim and full of worn-out wood and scratched stools. Only the pool table seemed well maintained, an oasis of smooth green felt under a single, bright lamp.

Doug ordered a beer and leaned against the bar. "Starting with the hard stuff, I see. No Mark?"

Alden swallowed the rest of his rum. "No sense wasting time." He shrugged. "He sounded pretty out of it when I called him."

"What kind of out of it?"

"With him, who knows? I'm surprised you made it."

"Why?"

"You said you had inventory."

"Starts tomorrow. My stuff's done. Any luck with the job search today? You said you were out when I called."

Someone wandered to the jukebox and played a power ballad that might have been attributed to any of several hair bands. Alden smiled and said, "No, I was just wandering around."

Doug nodded thoughtfully, then pointed a thumb over his shoulder and said, "Want to shoot some pool?"

Alden and Doug had come to this bar almost every Sunday for a least a year, and every time Alden's blasé answer was the same. "No, I never liked geometry."

"You're no good anyway," Doug said with a smile. "It's too damn easy." He had sipped a quarter of his beer and now chugged the rest. "Listen,

I can't really hang around tonight. Tiffany's expecting me." He winked. "Anniversary."

"How long?"

"A year tomorrow. Well, at midnight."

Alden grinned and shook his head. "You're so fucking whipped."

"Fuck you."

"No, thanks. I'd rather go without."

Doug slapped Alden on the shoulder and said, "You got that covered. I'll be working the day shift for inventory tomorrow and I'm sure it'll take a day or two to get back on the usual schedule. You coming?"

Alden glanced toward the door. "No, I'll probably hang out a while longer. Give me a call near the weekend."

"You got it," Doug said. "See you later."

Alden watched him go, then ordered another glass of rum.

It was after midnight when Alden parked his car in the covered space across from his townhouse. He noticed that the lawn needed to be mowed as he crossed it for his door. Aside from the grass, the subtle blue paint and white frames were in excellent condition; the development had only been built a few years ago.

Inside it was dark. The curtains were shut. The cool light of the street lamp outside could only slip through as a ghostly line on the tan carpet. Alden went into the kitchen and set his keys on the counter beside a bottle of spiced rum that was still mostly full. He opened the refrigerator and squinted.

Milk, but not enough for a bowl of cereal. Two bottles of water. A bag of cheese. Leftover pizza too old to eat. Pickles. Some salad dressing. He shut the door, grabbed the bottle of liquor, and wandered into the living room.

He picked up the remote and turned on the television. There was a late night talk show on a network station. He sat down of the couch and sighed. He was unscrewing the cap from the bottle of rum when his cell phone rang. The caller ID showed Doug's number.

"Hello?"

"Hey," Doug said with a shiver in his voice, "something's wrong."

Alden sat forward. "What?"

"Mark's mom just called me."

"And?"

"I'm leaving now for the hospital. Mark's mom called me. She found him passed out. She didn't think he was breathing. Couldn't wake him up."

Alden felt his cheeks go red in the darkness. "Where? Med center?"

"Yeah."

"I'll meet you there."

He rushed from the couch to the kitchen, took up his keys, and went outside. He backed his car out of the covered space and the tires chirped when he pulled away. *What the hell had happened?* Overdose, he thought. It had probably been an overdose. He drove fast. Cars parked on the side of the road went by in a blur. It had happened before. Mark's mother had found him then, too. Alden had made it to the hospital in time to be there when Mark had woken up, looking like shit and certainly feeling worse, but he'd been alive. He'd often looked weak from the drugs, but he was stubborn. Alden looked at his speedometer to see that he was nearing triple digits.

Ten minutes after leaving his townhouse, he parked his car near the emergency room entrance. The hospital had grown in recent years and the size was somehow intimidating, as if a larger structure meant more sickness and suffering. The bricks looked new, but they were probably a façade, and many of the windows were black in the late hour. Alden looked away from the bulk of the building and jogged to the emergency room's sliding glass doors. The fluorescent lights inside made his eyes sting. A nurse behind a desk nearby asked, "Can I help you?"

He ignored her and walked into the waiting room. Doug was there with Mark's mother—a plump woman with dyed orange hair and too much makeup. Her eyeliner had run onto her cheeks. Doug glanced at him when he entered, but seemed more inclined to look at the floor. There was an old man sitting in the corner reading a magazine.

"What happened?" Alden asked.

Doug slowly pulled himself away from Mark's mother. He had to peel her arms away from his gut. When he was free, he motioned with his head for Alden to follow him outside. The doors slid aside and they moved into the humid night air. Fog was gathering. They stepped away from the fluorescent shine into the slick darkness of the parking lot. The lamps overhead cast vague coronas against the faint stars.

"What happened?" Alden asked again.

"She thinks it was an overdose."

"Of what?"

"Heroin. She said there was some with him."

Alden looked down and scraped the edge of his shoe along the blacktop. "How is he?"

Doug opened his mouth, but hesitated. Alden looked at him with narrow eyes. The pause made his heart feel compressed and his breath stopped. Doug shook his head once, then turned around when his eyes went glossy. His hands were balled up.

Alden's knees started to shake and he thought he might fall. He reached back for some support, but there was nothing to grasp and he sat cross-legged on the ground.

"It's that bitch's fault," Doug whispered.

"Shut up."

"His mom said he still had a needle in his arm."

"Shut up."

Doug ran both hands through his short red hair and turned around. He looked over Alden toward the hospital doors. Alden stared at his own brown leather shoes, scuffed and worn and comfortable. There was a fresh scrape near the heel of the left one. It was vertical, short and wide. When did that happen? It didn't matter. He pushed the meandering thoughts away and forced himself to speak.

"We knew it was coming."

Doug looked down. "What?"

"Come on. We knew this was coming."

"We knew it could happen."

Alden clenched his jaw. "Oh, Jesus." He put his head in his hands and tried to keep his breath steady and deep, but it was awkward and shallow. His throat felt tight. He could feel the tears gathering against his eyelids. "Oh, Jesus Christ."

Doug huffed and stomped back into the hospital. Alden sat on the ground and tried to breathe in the heavy fog.

The sky was a deep blue when he parked across from his townhouse. Morning birds were singing to each other and Alden scowled. He slammed the car door and walked quickly across the lawn. He was gentler with the front door. His throat and face felt burnt. He went to the kitchen and drank from the faucet, then dragged his feet into the living room.

He wandered to the bookcase and crouched to examine the photo albums on the bottom shelf. He brushed his fingers along the wide spines, but he didn't move them. He lost his balance and sat on the floor, then leaned back and looked up at the ceiling. He sighed and closed his eyes. Mark's face glowed against his eyelids, full and healthy and young. His thick smile. His mop of curly blonde hair. The mischief flashing behind his eyes.

It was gone—all of it. There had been so much history between them. They'd grown up together. Mark had been at the hospital, only a few months old, for Alden's birth. He really had known Mark for his entire life. Now it meant nothing. It was gone, or if not, rendered meaningless by death. No, Alden thought, not meaningless. Mark's old influences remained. The history they'd built was still there, but it would never grow again.

Alden groaned and stood, but his legs still felt weak and he sat on the coffee table. He looked at the vague shape of the television in the dark, then at the shadows beneath it. He couldn't see it, but his videogame console was there, gathering dust in a compartment of the entertainment center. He hadn't used it in months—since Mark's addiction had gotten bad again. In better days they would spend hours sitting on the couch with the controllers, talking trash and wasting time. Doug joined them sometimes and they would organize pointless tournaments. Once in a while they wagered with dares or pocket change.

"No more," Alden whispered to himself. He stood and went back to the kitchen for another drink from the faucet. What an idiot Mark had been! How many times had he heard speeches from his mother, from Doug, from Alden himself? How many times had he nodded and agreed and promised to kick his habits? It didn't matter. It hadn't been enough. There was no gray area anymore.

It had slipped all the way into the black.

"Delayed," Doug muttered.

Alden frowned. "I know."

He felt uncomfortable. The funeral home was an old building beside a busy road. The old moss-colored carpet and wood grain walls made his head ache and the hiss of passing cars seemed somehow sacrilegious. He preferred the hiss of the small gathering, even if he disliked the people. It was as if they thought the wake gave them some significant connection to him, even though he'd probably never see them again. He wasn't sure how he would react if one more faceless uncle shook his hand seeking condolences.

"They didn't even care," Doug said, pulling at his red tie.

"They were just doing their job."

The wake had been delayed for an autopsy. Mark's death had been due to overdose as suspected and there had been a brief investigation. Alden had spoken with a police officer on the phone that morning; the call had come while he was getting dressed. Routine questions. What was his relationship with the departed? Did he know about Mark's addiction? Did he know where Mark had gotten the drugs? He had been evasive until he'd recognized the officer's last name—Tranis. They'd gone to college together. When he'd mentioned it the questioning had stopped and they'd engaged in a long conversation about how things had been recently, Mark's death aside. Tranis had heard about Alden's shooting in Franklin County. He was sorry it had happened that way. Alden had deflected the sympathy and asked about Mark's case. Tranis had been open.

Alden scratched his neck and looked at Doug. "Carfentanil."

"What?"

"It wasn't heroin."

"What are you talking about?"

Alden checked behind them. No one else was as close to the casket as they were. "It wasn't heroin, it was Carfentanil. The cop that looked into it called me and it turns out we went to college together. He told me what was in the report. It wasn't heroin."

"Who called you?"

"Kevin Tranis."

Doug whispered, "I got a call yesterday. What the hell is Carf-whatever?"

"Ever heard of fentanyl?"

Doug shook his head.

Alden looked back at the casket. Mark was still too thin and his blonde hair had been cut shorter. He didn't look right. Alden put a hand on Doug's shoulder and led him farther from their friend's corpse.

"Fentanyl's like morphine," he said.

"Okay."

"Carfentanil's like fentanyl, but worse. They use it on big animals."

"Like a horse tranquilizer?"

"Like an elephant tranquilizer."

Doug rubbed his cheek. "Where'd Mark get that?"

"Sometimes people mix heroin and fentanyl, but this wasn't that. Carfentanil is a lot stronger. No one uses it recreationally."

"What are you saying?"

Alden glanced at the room and pulled Doug into the corner. "The cops are putting a detective on it."

"Are you saying someone fucking killed him?"

Alden patted his hand in the air. "I don't know, but they're putting a detective on it. The drugs didn't appear out of nowhere, you know?"

Doug's face flushed and he shifted his weight back and forth between his feet. He had just begun to grind his teeth when they were interrupted.

"Aldy?" a tall man asked. "Doug?"

He was in his mid-twenties, but the acne on his face made Alden think most people would've thought him younger. His suit was cheap and didn't fit him very well—the shoulders were too tight and the sleeves too short.

"Vinny," Alden said with a genuine smile.

"How've you guys been?" he asked, then looked around. "This sucks, man."

Alden and Doug nodded. "Yeah," Doug said, his voice raspy and sharp.

There was a long silence before Vinny continued. "It's been a long time. I hadn't seen Mark since high school. You guys all stay tight?"

"Yeah."

"Sorry."

"Yeah."

Another silence, longer, passed between them until Vinny clasped his hands together in front of his chest and grinned. "Remember the napkin incident?"

Alden breathed a smile. "Of course."

The lunch line at their high school ended with a folding table covered in utensil trays, condiments, and napkin dispensers. Invariably, there were kids who forgot to take something from the table, especially napkins, so Mark took a handful with him to wherever he sat. Sometime during their junior year, Miss Hale noticed. The straight-backed, hollow-faced music teacher was outraged that students would waste supplies so readily. The next day, napkins were handed out with the trays by the kitchen staff, the dispensers out-of-reach.

When Mark sat at his table with his rationed napkins, he leaned across the faux wood and spoke in conspiratorial tones. Every day from that day forward, he and Alden and Doug and several others went without their napkins and handed them to Mark, who would smuggle them out to his car at the end of the day.

Sometime near the end of their senior year, when Miss Hale was supervising lunch, Mark and Alden left the cafeteria and went to Mark's car. He had stashed the napkins everywhere. They came from his glove compartment, his trunk, and his center console. They filled plastic bags, paper bags, and two of his mother's canvas totes.

Back inside, Mark took each container from Alden, and one by one he dumped them onto the scuffed brown lunch table. In moments there was a mountain of small white napkins that reached well above the heads of the kids sitting around it. Miss Hale noticed, screamed at them, and stormed out of the cafeteria in a swirl of layered black skirt. She returned with the principal—a plump, bald man with thick glasses and a love of plum-colored sport coats. He looked at the pile of napkins, then at Mark, then at Miss Hale, and he doubled over laughing.

"Classic," Vinny said.

"Awesome," Doug agreed.

"I heard he got into some bad shit."

"Yeah," Alden said.

"He used to be pretty straight-laced. What happened?"

Alden shrugged. "He met the wrong people, I guess."

Doug cracked his neck. "His girlfriend got him into it."

"Nasty shit," Vinny sighed. "Listen, you guys got cell phone numbers? Maybe we could get together sometime."

They exchanged numbers and Doug said, "I have to get out of here."

Vinny nodded and walked to the other side of the room. Alden said, "Yeah," and followed Doug toward the door. When they reached it, he stopped by the frame and glanced back at Mark's corpse.

"He looked less alive when he was breathing."

The next day was dry and hot and sunny. The graveyard gleamed with bright green grass and bleached tombstones. To the right, the steeple of the cathedral rose beyond the line of trees that separated the plots from the street, its lustrous white paint reaching for the blue sky. On the other three sides, beyond the black iron fence, sat the same crumbling houses he'd passed when he'd last been with Mark.

Alden wished the sun would disappear. It was supposed to be gray and rainy and cold. People were supposed to be bundled up in heavy black jackets under black umbrellas, but there were no jackets and no umbrellas. He felt hot and uncomfortable in his black wool suit. It was rented and it made him feel cheap and fake.

Doug stood beside him in an old blue suit that used to be his father's. It was worn, but it was honest. He wouldn't look at the casket suspended over the open earth. He stared at his feet or toward the road to his right, watching the cars pass by the brick cathedral on the nearby cross street.

The priest was talking, but Alden wasn't listening. He looked over the people around the casket. Mark's family had come—his mother and sister and his aunts and uncles and cousins. They huddled together on the other side of their dead relative, most weeping quietly. Alden didn't feel much like crying. He thought it was probably the heat and the sunlight. It didn't seem right or real.

Andrea hadn't come, Alden saw. How long had she and Mark been serious before the split? Three years? More? She should have come. He wondered where she was and what she was doing. He wondered who was with her. Maybe the dealer, like Doug had so often supposed. If so, she wasn't far away. The house where he and Doug had left Mark was only a block or two away.

The priest stopped talking. Mark's mother stepped forward and placed a bouquet of white flowers on the casket. Someone behind her sobbed and there was vague movement as someone consoled the griever. Alden looked at Doug.

"Let's go," Doug said.

They had lunch at Mark's mother's house. Alden and Doug were mostly unknown to Mark's relatives, so they snuck away after exchanging the required pleasantries and went upstairs to Mark's room. The oak paneling still needed to be replaced. The bed—just a mattress on the floor—was covered in tangled white sheets. A poster of Jim Morrison hung on the wall over a low dresser. The mirror on the back of the door was cracked at the bottom. The closet door was open and all of the bureau drawers were stacked on the floor. Someone had gone through them.

"What are we going to do?" Doug asked.

Alden leaned against the dresser. "What do you mean?"

"Someone fucking murdered him."

"Maybe."

"Maybe? Fuck maybe."

"Maybe, maybe not. Maybe it was a mistake, a mix up somewhere along the way. Maybe he thought he was buying heroin and they thought they were selling him heroin."

"You can't believe that."

Alden shook his head. "No, I don't, but it's possible."

"Someone has to pay for this."

"Maybe they will."

"*Fuck* maybe."

"They're putting a detective on it. Someone will find out what happened and if anyone needs to pay, they will."

"That's not guaranteed."

Alden's neck tingled with annoyance. "What do you want, Doug? Christ, he's dead, okay? There's nothing we can do. If they find out he was killed, fine, someone will be arrested and tried and whatever."

Doug slumped onto the mattress. "Not good enough." Alden watched him silently until he continued. "Someone has to pay for this. It was that fucking piece of shit dealer, I know it."

"How do you know that, huh? You don't *know* anything. Shut up about it, okay? Get over it. Cry or break something or whatever. Just do what you need to do and move on. Christ."

"Fuck you, Aldy. What are you doing? I haven't seen you really cry even once. Do you even fucking care?"

Alden stepped away from the dresser and leveled a finger at Doug, his eyes narrow and accusing. "Shut the hell up. You think I don't care? I care more than you could ever know. Mark was *my* best friend. *I'm* the one who knew him since he was born and *I'm* the one who tried to get him out of the shit he'd fallen into. So shut the hell up."

"You're the one?" Doug asked. "Really? Then why won't you fucking do something about it? Shit, man, someone killed him! He was murdered and you know it."

"Oh, and what do you want to do? You want to beat the shit out of his dealer because he died on some drug he wasn't even supposed to have?"

"I want to kill him."

Alden's arms fell at his sides. His face went slack. There had been no anger in Doug's voice when he'd said those words. *I want to kill him.* He was serious, but it had to be fueled by his usual hot-headedness.

"Don't be stupid," Alden said.

"He needs to pay for this."

"I'm leaving," Alden said as he opened the bedroom door. "Don't be stupid. Let it go."

"Fuck you."

Alden stepped into the hallway and shut the door. Was he really serious about this? Maybe he was now, but it would go away. He needed to spend a few days looking at it to get the right perspective. He was angry, but the anger would fade in time. He just needed time. They both needed time.

The phone was ringing. Alden groaned. It warbled like the birds that had kept him from falling asleep while the sun came up. He rolled over in bed and picked up the handset.

"Is this Alden?" asked an unfamiliar voice.

"Yeah."

"This is Barry from Hensen's. I was calling about the application you dropped off the other day."

Alden closed his eyes and sighed. "Oh, yeah. Listen, could I call you back tomorrow? Someone close passed away and we just had the funeral."

"Of course. I'm sorry. Call us back at your convenience. If you could ask for me when you call?"

"Barry."

"Yes, thank you."

Alden put the phone back in the charger and let his head fall back into the down pillow. He closed his eyes, but the desire for sleep had fled. He checked the clock. It was past noon. He threw the covers aside and swung his feet onto the floor. His head swam. He reached beside the bed and took the neck of a bottle in hand. He unscrewed the cap and took a long drink of cheap rum.

His shower was long and hot. He toweled off lazily and dressed in clothes he'd worn a few days before. They didn't really need to be washed yet; he'd only worn them once. He opened the refrigerator, but there was nothing to eat. He needed milk for cereal.

He went back to the bedroom and took a leather holster from the top drawer of his bureau. He slid it inside his waistband and snapped the loops to his belt. From beneath his bed he took his pistol—the .40 caliber Glock he'd bought before going to the academy—and slid it into the leather. He covered it with a wrinkled button-down shirt and looked in the mirror. It looked like he had two black eyes and he needed to shave.

The doorbell rang. He trotted down the stairs and saw through the narrow window beside the door that it was Doug. He rotated the deadbolt and opened the door. Doug stepped inside.

"You look like shit," Alden said.

"I haven't slept since my shift last night."

"You should get some sleep, then."

Doug scoffed and shook his head. "I can't sleep."

"You should try."

They walked into the kitchen and Doug opened the refrigerator. He moved a few things around, then asked, "How long's it been since you went the store? What do you eat around here?"

"I eat out."

Doug leaned against the counter in front of the window. Alden squinted in the afternoon light. "What's up?"

"I think we need to do something about Mark."

Alden rubbed his forehead and clucked once. "Every day? Are we going to do this every day now? I'm always going to tell you the same thing.

It's stupid and you're not thinking straight. You'll realize that when you calm down."

"I am calm."

"Not calm enough."

"You said to give it a few days. I did."

"No, you haven't given it any time at all. You just call me or ask me to meet you to talk about it. You need to spend some time thinking about it on your own."

"I always think about it."

"Then stop thinking about it. Take some vacation time and get away for a while. When was the last time you saw Tiffany?"

"This morning."

"See if she can get some time off. Go somewhere together. Get yourself straightened out about all of this."

Doug scoffed. "How can you be okay with this?"

"I saw it coming. It was going to happen someday."

"Fuck!" Doug slammed his fist against the counter and pushed away from it and out of the kitchen. Alden followed him into the living room and sat on the couch. Doug paced and said, "I'm going to do it."

"No, you won't."

"I will. I'm going to do it."

"You have your moments, but you're not that stupid."

Doug stopped. "Don't joke. I'm not joking."

"Okay. Relax. Sit down."

"No. I'm going to do it and I need your help."

Alden waved a hand in the air. "No way. You're not going to do anything. Are you listening to yourself? You really think you're going to murder someone and get away with it?"

"That's why I need your help. You know about this stuff, right? How many times have we talked about it?"

"About what? About robbing banks or how to mug people or how to do a hit?" Alden shook his head and snorted. "Come on. That's talk. Everybody talks. Talking isn't doing."

"But you really know how to do it."

Alden threw up his hands and sat back. "It's a fascination, Doug. Organized crime, crime treated as a real business, it interests me. There are people out there who love to study serial killers, but that doesn't mean they could go out and kill one person a month for the rest of their lives and never be caught. Christ, it's just a hobby." He sat forward and put his elbows on his knees. "It's academic."

"I'll do it without you."

"You're being foolish."

Doug folded his arms over his chest. "Why don't you fucking care? It's your fault!"

"What?" Alden said as he stood.

"We should've stayed."

"Like that would've made—"

"I wanted to stay!"

"Oh, and he couldn't have had the drugs in his pocket when he got back in my car for the ride home? Fuck you, Doug! My fault? He was dead whether we were there or not."

"You just keep telling yourself that."

"Get out."

"Help me."

"Get the hell out."

"Don't you want to know what happened? For sure?"

Alden stepped around the coffee table. "There's a detective looking into it. Who do you think he'd come looking for if that dealer got roughed up or ended up dead? You're not thinking."

"That's why I need your help."

"I'm not going to murder someone."

"Fine. Let's talk to him."

"The cops will do that."

"You know that for sure? You really think they care about a dead heroin addict?"

Alden stepped back and turned around. He looked through the open curtains at the small lawn behind the townhouse. Patches of it had turned brown in recent days. "It's not my fault," he said.

Doug paused. "I'm sorry I said that. I just want to know what really happened to him, you know?"

"Listen," Alden said, "I'll call Kevin Tranis and see what I can find out. He'll probably talk to me." He turned and looked at Doug. "Okay? Don't do anything stupid."

"What if he can't tell you anything?"

Alden looked at the blank television screen and his head moved back and forth slightly. "If they aren't moving on it, maybe I can convince them to dig deeper."

"What if they won't?"

"Let's not get ahead of ourselves," Alden said with white lips.

II

Doug shut the door behind him and Alden stepped into the kitchen again. He leaned against the stained countertop and stared between his feet at the cheap linoleum that tried to pass itself off as some kind of marble. His eyes followed the false veins. The air was still and hot, but he felt no inclination to turn on the air conditioner in the other room.

Mark's death hadn't been his fault. He was sure of that—as sure as he could be. How would it have made a difference? If his dealer, Tim or Tom or whatever he'd said on the phone, had really tried to make him overdose, would he have been put off by a car sitting outside? Maybe, but probably not.

Maybe?

It felt for a moment as if his heart was shrinking toward catastrophic implosion and he pressed a hand to his chest and doubled over. His legs felt suddenly insubstantial and he slid down against the cupboards to sit on the floor. His mouth opened in pain, then stayed wide with surprise and confusion. When the ache subsided he leaned his head back against the metal handle of a drawer and breathed a deep, wavering breath. He squinted at the rough white ceiling.

"Christ," he whispered.

It wasn't about staying outside of the house. It was about the seven years since Mark's first time using. He'd called it his "test flight." The thought made Alden's stomach turn. He'd tried hard to steer Mark away from all of it. Everyone had tried. There had been quiet conversations and thunderous arguments. Alden had once convinced him to see a counselor and start treatment with methadone, but it hadn't lasted more than a few weeks. Alden looked at the linoleum again. How long had it been since then? It had been in the winter, but warmer than usual. He remembered the hospital steps had been wet with cold rain. He hadn't bought his new car yet. It had to have been three or four years since then. There had never really been a turnaround. No progress, no upward motion. It had been one long slide downward, sometimes shockingly fast and sometimes agonizingly slow, but without pause.

Alden picked himself up slowly. His muscles felt watery. He had accepted the possibility that Mark could die, but he'd never expected it. He'd seen the signs of decay, but he hadn't done enough. He could have had Mark arrested for possession. He could have forced him to get clean. He could have done something more.

He clenched his teeth until his jaw ached. He stared at the single glass in the sink, its bottom sticky with a film of day-old rum. He tilted his head and blinked. He sniffed abruptly and walked to the living room, where he picked up his cell phone and dialed the police department where Tranis worked. He pressed numbers on the keypad to navigate the menu and enter the first few letters of the officer's name. A recorded message for Tranis's voicemail was the reply.

At the beep, Alden said, "Kevin, it's Alden. Listen, I was thinking, and now that things are quieting down a little around here, I was wondering if you might want to grab a beer sometime and catch up. Maybe talk a little shop. Let me know."

He ended the call and fell back onto the couch. After a minute or two he felt a bead of sweat break free from his hairline and drop into his eyebrow. He got up and turned on the air conditioner. For a long time he stood in front of the vents, letting the cool air dry the sweat on his face until the skin felt tight and gritty.

In the kitchen he picked up his keys. He needed groceries.

Alden's cell phone rang while he was looking at a can of vegetable soup. He shifted the red basket—still mostly empty—to his other hand and took the phone from his belt. He flipped it open and answered.

"Hello."

"Alden, hey, it's Kevin. I got your message."

"Hey, what's up?"

"I just wanted to let you know that a beer sounds pretty good. I'm busy tonight, but I'm working first shift for the rest of the month, so I'll be free tomorrow night."

Alden forced a smile so his voice would send it and said, "Great! Have any place in mind?"

"RJ's has free wings tomorrow."

"Sounds good. What time is best?"

"How's twenty-one hundred?"

"Works for me. I'll see you there."

"Cool. It's a plan."

Alden flipped his phone shut and returned it to the plastic holder on his belt. He picked up the can of vegetable soup and put it in the basket, then took several more cans at random. He didn't care what they would taste like. The appraising looks of the shoppers around him seemed pretentious, as if there was no more important a decision than what bag of bread to buy. It made the blood in Alden's cheeks feel hot and a twist of mild panic climbed from the pit of his stomach to the front of his chest. What was wrong? He couldn't identify the source of his discomfort, but the sensations grew rapidly and he hurried toward the checkout lanes.

He forced another smile for the cashier—a skinny teenager wearing too much lip gloss and a nametag that read, "Aimée." She had drawn the accent with a marker.

He placed his five cans of soup and the half gallon of milk on the conveyer and looked back toward the aisles. Things looked fuzzy in the distance and he blinked. He swiped his debit card and entered his PIN while the cashier scanned his items and placed them into a plastic bag. Through the large windows at the front of the store he could see a young couple putting their groceries into a white minivan.

"Do you want cash back?"

Alden's head snapped back to the cashier and he said, "What?"

"Do you want cash back?"

"Uh, no, thanks."

"You just have to hit the button."

"Sorry," he said.

He declined cash back on the card reader's touch screen and stared at the cashier's hand as it hovered over the receipt printer, her fingers twitching impatiently. She snatched up the receipt when it emerged and shoved it into his grocery bag without looking.

He took up the bag and offered an unacknowledged, "Thanks."

Outside, he took a deep breath of the heavy, humid air. His heart was beating fast and the back of his head was starting to ache. The glare from the cars in the parking lot made him squint to the point of near blindness. He fumbled his keys out of his pocket and sat in the driver's seat, letting the grocery bag fall onto the floor on the passenger side. His breath was coming fast. As he put the key in the ignition and turned on the car, the tips of his fingers began to tingle. He shook his head and exhaled a short groan.

"Just get home."

He left the parking lot for the street. He waited at a traffic light to turn onto Route 2, busy even in the middle of a weekday afternoon. When the light changed to green he turned and started toward the Interstate, but his eyes were fixed forward and he drove past the onramp, heading toward the city. Route 2 would eventually turn into Main Street.

The road turned and dipped and narrowed, sending him downhill toward the taller buildings of downtown. The lake beyond flashed white under the sun. In the city he turned north. He followed the street until the bustle was left behind, replaced by tiny houses and old duplexes, many showing the first signs of disrepair. A few children were riding rusty bicycles on the side of the street and he slowed as he passed them, but didn't look. His eyes were still fixed ahead.

He turned left onto a narrow side street and weaved his way among cars parked on either side of the road. He looked right, and between the houses and their dying lawns he saw the bright glare of headstones. Ahead he could see the steeple of Saint Joseph's rising above the cracked roofs.

He turned again and the cemetery came into view on his right. It was long and thick with old, crack granite. The black iron fence that surrounded it glowed dark gray in the sunlight, falling in and out of shadow beneath the widely-spaced trees inside. He stopped the car at the curb near the gate and got out.

He walked through the gate slowly. The grass beneath his shoes was green, but it sounded dry and he could feel it cracking as he moved. At the far end of the cemetery he watched a shadow drift over the headstones, then disappear as a cloud passed overhead. A breeze swirled over the plots, occasionally snapping with a strong gust that made his shirt cling to his back.

He walked to Mark's grave. The gray granite headstone was small, just a block of stone pressed into the earth. Alden looked at it and shoved his hands into his pockets. It was engraved with his friend's name and the dates of his birth and death. No one seemed to want epitaphs anymore, Alden thought, but Mark should have had one. It was more than the grave of an addict. It had to be more than that.

Alden turned and looked north. The house where he'd left Mark couldn't have been much more than a quarter mile from where he stood. He wondered if the dealer was there now. What would he be doing? Watching television? Checking his e-mail? Making a phone call? Sleeping with Andrea?

Alden turned back to Mark's headstone. Doug was being foolish concerning the dealer. There was no doubt about that. He was more upset than Alden had expected, but the pain would fade in time. His senseless bloodlust was a temporary lack of reason, but Doug had been right about one thing. There were answers waiting to be found and Mark deserved more than a tiny piece of granite in the grass.

He took his cell phone from its holder and dialed Doug. It rang only once before he heard, "What's up?"

"I'm meeting Kevin tomorrow night," Alden said. "Are you working?"

"Yeah, I start at ten."

"Keep your phone on. I'll call you when I know something."

"Oh, okay."

"Talk to you then."

Alden arrived at the bar just before nine o'clock. It was dimly lit and the floor sat below the level of the door. He moved down the steps into the interior of old wood. The weather outside was pleasant and the place seemed busy for a weekday. Tranis was at a small table on the wall opposite the bar, a half-empty glass of beer and a basket of wings in front of him. Alden sat in the other chair and smiled.

"How's it going?" Tranis asked.

"It's going. You?"

"Same. Something to drink?"

"Sure."

Tranis waved at a waitress and she came to their table.

"Rum with a twist of lime?" Alden asked.

"On the rocks?"

"Neat, thanks."

Tranis turned a wing over in his fingers and said, "Sorry about your friend. Were you close?"

Alden gave a small shrug and said, "Not very. We had a falling out after high school. I'm good friends with a guy who's pretty broken up about it. They were closer."

"The guy you were with when you dropped him off?"

"Yeah. We were hanging out when Mark called for a ride, so we picked him up and dropped him off on our way to eat."

"Too bad."

"He got himself into it, you know?"

Tranis nodded. "I hear that. Still, you've had it pretty rough lately, from what I hear. Didn't go so well up north."

"Oh," Alden said, "that. Yeah, it was pretty hairy."

"I just read it in the papers. What the hell happened?"

"It was supposed to be a domestic, but it turned out his girlfriend had made a false report because she thought he was cheating on her." Alden grabbed a wing and smiled his thanks to the waitress as she delivered his drink. "My backup was at least fifteen minutes away. You know how it is out there."

"And you were primary?"

Alden finished the wing and sipped the rum. "I was closest. I'd only been on my own for a couple of weeks. Anyway, I show up at this place, this little house in the middle of nowhere in the woods. The kind of place you'd expect. Rusted out cars on the lawn next to the driveway, like that."

"Nice."

"Yeah, very classy. This guy was standing on the porch, drunk off his ass. I got out and he came off the porch. I told him to stop, but he kept coming, so I got my OC out in case he got too close. Of course he did, swearing at me to get off his property, telling me he was going to kick my ass if I didn't mind my own business. I told him to stop again and he didn't, so I hit him with the OC. It was a good stream—right to the eyes. He howled like mad."

Tranis smiled.

"But he didn't stop," Alden continued. "His eyes were shut tight, but he kept coming. I'm not a very big guy and this guy was huge. Six feet at least and probably close to three hundred pounds. He latched onto me good and wouldn't let go. He smelled horrible. His breath probably would've wilted flowers. We went to the ground and it got messy."

"Shit."

Alden took another drink. "I lost my spray and tried to get him off of me. I kneed him in the ribs and tried to get to his throat, and that might've worked, but I felt him going for my gun. I put both hands on it, but he was big. I was just praying that the retention would do its job, but he was trying to hit me with his other hand and I didn't do a very good job of pushing my weapon. I felt the retention pop and I knew he was going to get it."

Tranis was shaking his head.

"I was out of time," Alden said, "so I used my off hand to drop the mag. I figured it would be better if he had one round instead of fourteen. After I hit the release, I let him have it. He pushed himself back once he had the gun and I kicked him away. He fell over and had a hard time getting up. I went for my backup. I had a little five-shot .357 at my ankle. I'd just cleared the holster when he fired. He missed and I didn't."

"No shit? And they fired you for that."

"They have a policy against backups."

"You'd think they might've let it slide, considering."

Alden smirked. "They may have talked to me about it once before, off the record. I agreed to keep it at home."

"Oh," Tranis said. "Still, come on. You could be dead."

"Could be."

"How was the shrink?"

"They fired me. I didn't go."

"You okay with that?"

Alden scoffed. "Fuck yes. The guy tried to kill me. He made a decision to get that drunk. He made a decision to go for my gun. He wanted a fight and he got one. He lost. Why should I be upset about that?"

"A guy here had a shooting a month ago and he's still out. No one even got hit."

"What the hell is that about?" Alden asked. "What are these guys thinking? Why get into a job if you can't handle it? Shit happens."

"I hear that," Tranis said.

He raised his beer and Alden clinked his glass of rum against it. They both drank and Tranis asked, "What are you doing now?"

"Looking for work."

"Anything interesting?"

"Not really. What about you? Liking the job?"

Tranis nodded enthusiastically. "Yeah, I love it."

"I thought you wanted to go federal."

"I did, but I like the city and I kind of want to stay. I'd like to break into the detective bureau eventually, but I need more time on the street."

Alden's heart leapt and began to beat hard against his chest. He sensed the opening in the conversation, the junction at which he could turn it to his ends. He felt suddenly nervous and was afraid that his hands might start to shake, so he picked up another wing.

"Is that why you were the one looking into the overdose?" Alden asked with a wry smile. "Trying to brown-nose your way in?"

Tranis grinned. "No, it would've stopped with me if the toxicology report hadn't been so strange. That's why the detective was on it."

"Was on it? They took him off?"

"It dried up, I guess."

Alden forced his eyebrows up in a look a surprise. "Did he even talk to whoever lives at that house? Where I dropped Mark off?"

"Yeah, but it must've been nothing."

"I told you that was probably his dealer."

"Don't look at me," Tranis said with a raised hand. "I didn't call it off and I don't know what was said in the interview."

"Oh, so they interviewed the guy, at least."

"Yeah, they talked to him and I'm pretty sure they even looked through his place, but nothing happened. It's cold now, I think."

Alden chewed and took deep, slow breaths through his nose. Had it been that easy? He looked into Tranis's eyes and hoped the movement of his jaw would cover the brief grimace he was unable to contain. He dropped the bone onto a napkin and said, "Well, that sucks."

"Yeah," Tranis said. "Sorry, man."

Alden tried to replicate the shrug he'd given earlier, but he wasn't sure it was convincing. He needed to change the topic. If talk about Mark was the thing that Tranis remembered about this conversation, it could mean trouble if Doug went to question the dealer.

"So," Alden said, "if you get a detective spot, what next?"

"I dunno. Maybe something more specialized, like CUSI or something. I wouldn't mind sticking it to some of those sickos."

"I don't know if I could handle that. I can see 'excessive force' somewhere in the paper if I had to deal with that stuff. Working sex crimes wouldn't be good for my health."

Tranis took a sip of his beer. "I responded to a rape a while back. Didn't bother me much, but I definitely wanted to nail the guy that did it. I could use that kind of motivation every day."

Alden canted his head in consideration and said, "I hadn't really thought about it that way, but you're probably right. It would be quite a reason to get out of bed in the morning." He finished his rum. "If you could ever get to sleep at night."

Tranis nodded. "What kind of work are you looking for?"

"Well, policing is out, so I'm not really sure. The CJ degree doesn't give me a lot of options."

"What about some kind of courtroom work?"

"Like what?"

"I don't know. Victim's advocate or something, maybe."

Alden sneered slightly. "Doesn't interest me much. Nothing does, at the moment. I've applied at a few places. A bookshop called me back yesterday, but I don't know if I really want to do that. Nothing seems exciting anymore."

"Yeah, well, I guess the chances of being shot at are a little slimmer in that line of work, even if it is boring."

"That's the problem," Alden said. "After that happened, everything just got dull, like it didn't really matter much. I should've expected that, I suppose, and it'll probably go away after a while. It hasn't been very long and, to be honest, I kind of miss the feeling."

"Of being shot at?"

"Sort of," Alden said, taking another wing from the basket. "It's hard to describe. It wasn't being shot at, exactly. It was just that it was dangerous, or that it was as dangerous as it was. I could've died from the bullet, but I don't think it's about the source of the danger. It's the intensity."

Tranis gave him a blank look. "You should take up skydiving or something."

"That wouldn't do it. Skydiving is a hobby. It could be dangerous if something went wrong, but you're not fighting for your life." Alden bit into the wing. "I don't know," he said as he chewed. "I can't really explain it."

"No, I think I get it," Tranis said. "You're insane."

They both smiled, then laughed. The waitress returned and Tranis ordered another beer. Alden slid his empty glass to the edge of the table for her and said, "I'll have another, thanks."

He turned back to Tranis and asked, "So what are you up to now, other than work?"

"I'm pretty big into motorcycles, actually. Just bought an old Harley a few weeks ago. I should have it running soon. Do you ride?"

"Never learned."

"You should. It's a blast, I'm telling you."

"I've thought about it. I just never seem to find the time."

Tranis grinned. "You've got it now, right? You should definitely check it out. I think you'd love it."

Alden smiled, but behind the expression there was no substance. He felt a void growing among his insides, as if the small moment of enjoyment—the chuckle they had shared—had been twisted into insignificance. The pallor he had tried to describe had swirled up from beneath his stomach and into his mind. Everything seemed dull and gray; excitement was beyond reach.

"Don't you have to register for the classes way in advance?" he asked, lustfully seeking to destroy any possibility of appeasing Tranis.

"Yeah, but you don't have to go through the class. A lot of people just think that's the easiest way."

"I'll have to look into it."

When their drinks came, Alden drank the rum down in one long gulp, leaving the twist of lime tangled in amber-colored residue at the bottom of the glass.

"Wow," Tranis said.

Alden smirked, but his eyes didn't show it. "That's it for me."

"What you about? What have you been up to, aside from looking for a new job?"

Burying my friend, Alden wanted to say, but he shrugged one shoulder and said, "Not much. I've been reading a lot. I never had the time before."

"That why you went for the bookstore?"

"Yeah."

Tranis's cell phone sounded a monotonous tune, barely audible over the din of the bar. He pulled it from his pocket and answered.

"Hey," he said. "Yeah, I'm out with that guy from college." There was a pause. "Yeah, I can do that. Okay. I'll see you soon."

Alden raised his eyebrows.

"My fiancée," Tranis explained with a frown. He took a few large swallows of beer. "Her mom's in the hospital with cancer. I kind of have to go."

"That's cool," Alden said. "It's no problem. We should hang out again sometime."

"Yeah, definitely," Tranis said as he stood.

Alden got up as well and fished some cash from his pocket. He counted out a few bills and tossed them on the table.

"I got it."

"You sure?" Tranis asked.

He nodded and they shook hands.

"I'll see you later," Alden said. "Take care."

"Yeah, you bet. Sorry I have to run. See you."

Alden watched Tranis take the wooden steps to the door and walk outside. He breathed a long sigh, relieved to be without company, and moved into the cool night air. A breeze blew up from the lake and it felt soothing on his cheeks as he made his way down the hill toward his car. He trotted over a cross street when the traffic light turned red and reached into his pocket for his car's remote.

The silver sedan gave a haughty honk and the headlights flashed twice. He sat inside and closed the door. The absence of the breeze made the air feel stagnant and his cheeks felt hot again. He started the car and swiveled one of the air conditioning vents toward his face. A raspy ballad was playing on the radio and he changed the station. A commercial.

He put the car in reverse and backed out of the space. He looked up the hill, past the line of neon-lit bars and the shadowy park opposite. He turned the corner and drove around the block, heading north, away from downtown. He didn't feel like going home.

Alden turned the lights off as he brought the car to the opposite side of the street. He turned the key and let it coast for a few seconds before using the hand brake to stop. He was almost to the corner. Through the passenger window he could see the stoop of the apartment house glowing a cool blue in the light of a tall, gray streetlamp. The porch beyond the steps was shadowed black, but carved into the darkness were bright rectangles of dirty yellow light. Someone was moving inside—a man, overweight and wearing glasses.

Another figure stood. A woman—Andrea. Her dark, curly hair bounced around her shoulders as she hugged him, then kissed him. He slid his hands down her back and out-of-view.

Alden's hands tightened on the steering wheel. His heart ached and swirled into some deep recess of his chest. The pain stole his breath and blurred his vision, but he couldn't stop looking through the windows of the little apartment house. He grimaced and his teeth clenched. He bit the side of his tongue and tasted blood.

The man inside was smiling. Andrea was laughing. He'd told a joke. It had probably been crude. Might it have been about Mark? Alden opened his mouth and sucked in a great breath. A headache had begun behind his eyes. He glanced into the backseat, then stared at the silver door handle. Mark had been the last person to touch it. Alden clawed at his chest, trying to pull his heart forward as it lurched again, falling deeper and growing smaller. His fingertips tingled. His toes felt numb in his sneakers. His lungs shuddered as he drew breath and he blinked away tears.

He looked at the apartment house again. Andrea and the man were gone. Alden sobbed once, then sat up straight. In an instant it all turned. The dull fog that had enveloped his senses was suddenly tinted red and his heart surged back into place, beating fast and hot. He blinked again and wiped his eyes with his sleeve. He shook his head and took several fast, steady breaths. The framed yellow lights were still empty. He took a deep breath, then exhaled as slowly as he could. The air rattled in his throat.

He became aware of the pressure behind his right hip, where his pistol was holstered inside the waistband of his jeans. He closed his eyes and saw Tranis's mouth moving, telling him again, "It's cold now, I think." He saw himself knocking on the door, pistol in hand, the slide pressed into the back of his right thigh. The door opened and he pushed the man inside. He kicked the door shut behind him and forced the man onto his knees. He stepped around him and fired a single shot. Andrea appeared in a doorframe. She screamed and ran.

Alden opened his eyes. That fantasy served no purpose, and if made real, would provide no real satisfaction. It would accomplish nothing. He didn't know anything yet.

He turned the key and turned on the headlights. As he pulled away from the curb he took his cell phone from its holder and dialed Doug.

"Hey."

"Do you work tomorrow?" Alden asked.

"Yeah. I start at ten again."

"Stop by my place before you go in."

"Okay," Doug said. "Did you meet with that cop?"

"Yeah. Just left. I'll tell you about it tomorrow."

"Oh, come on. What did he say? Did they find out anything about Mark yet?"

"He thinks they've stopped looking."

There was a pause before Doug spoke again. Alden could hear the tightness of excitement in his voice when he did. "So we'll talk to this guy?"

"We'll discuss it tomorrow."

"We at least have to talk to him. Come on—"

"Tomorrow," Alden said. "Tomorrow, okay?"

"Okay."

Alden closed the phone and tossed it onto the passenger seat. In the rear view mirror he saw the cemetery, but he didn't remember passing it.

Doug came around a few hours before his shift was supposed to start. Alden met him at the door. He had been pacing in the kitchen and drinking rum neat. They sat in the living room, Doug in an old armchair and Alden on the couch.

"So, he thought they called off the dogs," Doug said with a triumphant grin.

Alden nodded slowly. "I'm sure it's not high on the list."

Doug leaned forward and rubbed his hands together. "That means we get to talk to this guy, right?"

"What do you want to ask him?"

"I want to find out about Mark."

"Right, but what do you want to ask him? What would your first question be? How would you phrase it?"

"What the fuck are you talking about?"

Alden looked away, disgusted. Doug could be so ignorant, so crude. He was still angry and it was blinding him, but why should that be a surprise? Something was always blinding him. He talked about questioning someone who might have murdered Mark like he would've criticized someone who had cut him off in traffic. The tone was the same. Didn't he see the difference?

"What are you talking about?" Doug demanded again.

"Andrea is with him. She was with him last night."

"So you think he was jealous? You think that's why?"

"We don't know anything."

Doug threw up his hands, then slapped his knees. "You keep saying that. 'We don't know anything,' or 'you don't know anything.' How are we going to find out, huh? We have to talk to him."

Alden put his elbows on his knees and said, "Yes."

Doug's eyes widened. "Really?"

"He deserves answers."

"Damn right."

"We need to think," Alden said. "We need to have a plan."

"We have a plan. We show up and ask him what the hell happened. We ask him if he gave Mark the drugs."

Alden brought his hands to his forehead, then ran his fingers through his hair. "No," he said softly, "we need a real plan. All the little details. We need to be careful. We might need to go to the police and they'll want an explanation. They'll want to know why we were there and how we know what we know."

"The police? Why would we need the police? If he tells us he killed Mark, we fuckin' off the guy."

"How?"

"What?"

"How? How would we off the guy?"

Doug shrugged. "Who cares?"

"The detective who'll investigate it will care. He'll care about motive. He'll care about the time of death. He'll care about the fibers and the fingerprints you left behind." Alden sat up straight. "Then he'll care about your alibi, and when he breaks apart the brittle story you put together at the interrogation table, he'll care about how you write your admission."

Doug's mouth hung open for a moment before he said, "That's why I need you."

"We've been over this. It's academic. If you want to talk to this guy, fine, but we're not killing anybody."

"What if he says he did it?"

"Then we go to the cops. We give our statements and they'll put more into the investigation."

"As much as they did last time? What if this guy just tells them he never said what he said? What can they do? Are they going to lock him up on our word?"

Alden looked down at the carpet. "Probably not."

"And if he says he did it, how is it any different than the other guy? If he killed Mark, how is he any different than the guy who tried to kill you, huh? He isn't. He's just the same and he deserves to go the same way, and you know it. Come on! If anything, he's worse. He des—"

"Shut up," Alden said. "Are you serious? You haven't let this drop. Are you serious about this? Do you really think that killing this guy will make any difference in how you feel?"

"Maybe not, but this is for Mark, not me."

"That's bullshit. This is for you."

Doug threw out his arms. "So what if it is?"

"If it is, then it matters if this guy's death would make you feel better. That's what it's about, right? Feeling better? Feeling like you did something to help Mark, even if it was after the end?"

Doug twisted his head around and looked out the window. There was still deep blue light in the western sky. After several seconds, he said, "You feel guilty, too."

"I tried to help him."

"Me, too, but he's dead."

"Yeah."

Doug stared at his hands. "You want this, too. You must want this, too. Don't you? Don't you want it to balance out? I mean, how can you be so calm about it? How can you do nothing?"

"I can't," Alden said.

"I've never wanted to do something like this before. I mean, I've been pissed off, whatever, but not like this."

"You feel like someone took something from you. Not Mark. Something deeper. Something that was part of you. You don't feel whole."

"Y-yeah."

Alden nodded. "Me, too."

"I don't want to feel this way anymore."

"Neither do I."

"So, what do we do?" Doug asked.

Alden sat back against the couch cushions and looked up at the ceiling. "It could've been a mistake."

"Let's talk to him."

"We will."

"And if he killed him?"

Alden sat forward and looked Doug in the eye. "If we do this—if he says that and we do this—we have to do it right."

Doug nodded once, then whispered, "Okay."

"You'll have to listen to me and do what I say."

"Okay."

"You'll have to trust me."

"Come on. How long have we known each other?"

"You'll have to listen to me and not what's in your head. Can you do that? Do you think you'll be able to do that?"

"Yeah," Doug said. "Yeah."

Alden bit his lip. "I need to think. Do you work tomorrow?"

"No."

"Can you stop by in the afternoon?"

"Sure."

"Okay, do that. Just give me a call before you get here."

"You really want to do this?" Doug asked.

"I don't know if I can answer that."

Doug stood up and walked toward the kitchen. "I'll call you tomorrow before I leave, okay?"

"Okay."

Alden woke just after noon. The patch of sunlight shining on the white wall made the room glow in his sleep-hazy eyes. He sat up and ran a hand through his hair. The heat that had burned in his chest was gone; watching Andrea and the dealer seemed years behind him. He stood with a little groan and gathered some clothes.

His cell phone rang while he was in the shower, but he didn't rush. He checked his voicemail after he had dressed.

"It's Doug. I'm on my way."

He erased the message and went to the kitchen. He'd only eaten half of the vegetable soup he'd made last night. He took the bowl from the refrigerator and heated it in the microwave. Doug knocked while he was washing the bowl. Alden dried his hands and opened the door.

"Hey," Doug said. "What's up?"

Alden closed the door and said, "I don't think we should do this."

"I thought you were good to go."

They moved into the living room and Alden said, "I don't know what I was thinking. I saw Andrea at that guy's house and, I don't know." He shook his head. "I don't know."

"Fuck that," Doug said. "You want to know. You want to know what happened to Mark as much as I do. I know you do. Come on! You said I'd calm down. You said I'd get over it. Well, I'm not over it. I still want to do it. I'm serious about this and I'll do it without you."

Alden sank into the couch. "I do want to know, but let's assume this guy actually did give him that drug to kill him. Then what? You want to kill him, but there's no way I'm going to murder someone. How would we be different?"

Doug scoffed. "How would we be different? We'd have killed him to give Mark a little justice. He killed Mark so he could fuck his girlfriend. It's totally different."

Alden sighed and stared at the blank television screen. "I just don't think I could do it."

"You've already done it. You've done it and it didn't bother you at all. You were perfectly fine with it."

"He was trying to kill me."

"This guy already killed Mark."

"We don't know that."

"Let's fucking *assume*."

"Assume a truth that you think would justify murder? That's a pretty big assumption, don't you think?" Alden leaned forward. "And how do you think you're going to get the truth out of him? I doubt he's going to smile and admit to a murder because we asked politely."

"That's why I need you. You know how to question people, right? He'll talk to you."

"This is a little different than a field interview."

Doug threw up his arms. "Then we'll beat the shit out of him until he tells us the truth."

"And admits to something he didn't do to stop the beating. Jesus, Doug, you want to torture a guy for no reason? Because that's what you're saying. You have nothing on this guy, just a suspicion, and you want to kick him around until he says what you want to hear."

"Do you *really* think he didn't know what he was giving to Mark?"

Alden shook his head. "No."

"Then there you go."

"Christ."

Doug stopped pacing and stared toward the kitchen. "Remember the trip to the water park?" he asked.

"What?"

"The trip to the water park in New York. Remember that?"

Mark's parents had once taken them to a tourist town in New York State. They gave Alden, Mark, and Doug their own room for the week. How old had he been? Eleven or twelve, probably. They went to a water park for a few days, then an amusement park. They spent their evenings in town at one of the local arcades, rolls of quarters sagging the pockets of their shorts.

Once, when they stopped for a picnic lunch, Mark left his camouflage hat behind. They drove back to the picnic area to look for it, but it had disappeared. Mark exclaimed, "We'll never be able to find it! It's camouflage!" It had become an inside joke between them.

Alden smirked and said, "Yeah, I remember that."

"Well," Doug snapped, "he's rotting in a graveyard. He's dead because this guy was killing him with the heroin and because his guy wanted to fuck his girlfriend. He's dead and it's over. No more water parks, or napkin piles, or late-night videogame competitions. Someone murdered him and no one's ever going to pay for it. Can you live with that? Because I can't. I won't. I owe him more than that and so do you."

No one's ever going to pay for it. That was probably true. Drugs could've been mixed up. It might not be likely, but it could be the truth. If the detective couldn't find anything on the dealer, chances were slim that he would spend any more time on the investigation. The truth would be left undiscovered. Could he live with that?

Alden looked at the ceiling. He thought about the bottle of rum in his cupboard, almost empty. No, he probably couldn't live with that for very long. His family was distant and he hadn't dated in a while. With Mark gone, Doug was the only person with whom he had any connection. Was it the loneliness more than the loss? Was he so selfish?

"I can't live with that, either," Alden said.

"So?"

"When's your next day off?"

"Tomorrow," Doug said. "This is my weekend."

"Come back tomorrow."

"So we're on?"

A surge of sweat made Alden's hands feel sticky, but his voice was steady when he said, "We're on."

Doug left and Alden turned on the television. The news was on and he changed the station. He didn't watch it—it was just for the background noise. Instead he went to the bookshelf beside his chair. He took down a thin paperback and returned to the couch. The cover showed a man in a yellow suit and hat holding a suppressed pistol. The figure was superimposed over the shape of a dead body colored red. The subtitle called it a "technical manual." Alden smirked. How many times had he read it? He couldn't remember. It had been the hook that had pulled him into his fascination with crime as a career. For most it was an amateur's impulsive grab at something—cash or power or exhilaration. There were very few professionals.

He flipped through the thin book. Alden only knew of one person who'd used it as a manual. That guy had ended up in prison for a triple homicide, but he'd been arrested before. He wasn't a professional, was he? He'd called the man who'd hired him from a hotel where he'd booked a room. It was an amateur's mistake.

Even with such a crime, rumors circulated that the book hadn't been written as a serious "technical manual" at all, but had been put together by some bored woman who'd intended to write a novel. Maybe that was true, but Alden had always had a knack for pulling the useful bits of information from sources filled with unusable fiction. It was a talent he'd never been able to explain. His mind seemed to do it without his direction.

What interested him most was a chapter about putting together a suppressor. Alden skimmed a few lines of text and read a list of items needed for the construction. He had none of them, but there were easier ways to make suppressors. He'd once seen instructions that made use of a pipe and several bottle caps, though he was skeptical about its effectiveness.

He put the book on the coffee table and stood. He stretched and groaned. He felt tired, exhausted. He turned off the television and went upstairs for a nap. Sleeping in the afternoon would mean being awake all night, but that didn't matter. He would've been awake all night anyway.

Alden opened his eyes and looked at the clock. He'd slept through the night. What, fifteen hours? He blinked and sat up. The blue light spilling into the room around the curtains probably meant that the sun hadn't quite cleared the horizon yet. He thought he should've felt groggy, but he was fully awake, his mind already clear and sharp.

He took a long, hot shower and stared at himself in the mirror. His cheeks showed a few days' stubble and he turned on his electric razor, but turned it off and set it down before it touched his face. It would be best to stop shaving for a while. He put the razor under the sink.

He made himself a simple breakfast of bland cereal, but it was nice to have the food and fresh milk. It was brighter outside and the light had turned from blue to gold. As he rinsed his bowl he whispered to himself, "You're not really going to do this, are you?" He set the bowl on his dish rack. *Are you?* He would question the dealer, but would he kill him? If this Tom or Tim admitted to Mark's murder, if he flaunted the fact in front of them as some prideful boast, what would he, Alden, do about it? What *could* he do? That was what really mattered, wasn't it? His capabilities would be as important as his knowledge. Therein was the question. Where were his limits?

He walked out of the kitchen, through the living room, and into the tiny office in the corner of the townhouse. He sat in the high-backed chair and turned on his computer. While it booted up, he slid a pad of lined paper next to the mouse pad and took up a pen. He clicked the point out and in a few times and then started several lists. He divided things into categories, assigning each more space on the page than it would probably require. They needed to consider everything, from weapons—by design or improvisation— and other equipment to things like clothing and transportation.

When the operating system had loaded, he launched his web browser and ran several searches. He began with an online legal library where he looked up several cases involving contract killers, including the guy who had used the "technical manual" as his guide. As he found them, he sent them to his printer. In every case the killer or killers had been convicted; Alden wanted to know what mistakes they'd made. With the printer whirring, he began trying various web pages for documents regarding improvised suppressors. He found several files in a matter of minutes, all of which he queued for printing behind the legal cases. He next visited the website for the largest local newspaper and ran a search of its classifieds. He found the section he was looking for under the heading *Hunting/Fishing*. There was a listing for some .45 caliber ammunition, another for a compound bow, a third that requested military items for a buyer, and a fourth for a 12-gauge Winchester shotgun with a full set of chokes. Alden frowned. There was nothing he could use.

He slid his chair to the printer. He sorted out the documents, tapped them on the desk to straighten them out, and stapled them. He set them in neat piles—one for the legal documents and another for the suppressors. Back at the computer, he cleared his browser's history and deleted his cookies and temporary files. He would need to do a complete format later, when things were done. It would have to be with the proper software, the kind that overwrote the hard disk several times. He immediately added that software to his list, then put down the pen and stood. The rest of the day's work would take more effort.

He went to the bathroom and looked in the mirror. The stubble on his cheeks wasn't very noticeable and it didn't detract much from the business-casual professionalism of his button-down shirt and slacks. It might even add to the image he wanted to convey, but that would come later, during business hours. It was still early, but Mark's mother had always jumped out of bed before the sun had risen. Alden called her on his cell phone.

"Hello?" she answered, sounding alert as expected.

"Hey, Misses Paladino, it's Alden."

"Oh, hello, honey. How are you?"

"All right, I guess. I was wondering if I could ask you a favor?"

"Of course, hon."

"Do you still have Mark's things? His phone?"

There was a brief pause before she replied, "I think so."

"It's just, well, there was a guy he was supposed to introduce me to," Alden lied, "about a job. I was wondering if I could check his phone to get the number, if that's okay."

"Oh, sure, that's fine."

"Are you leaving for work soon?"

"No," she said, "not for a little while."

"Could I stop by on my way to today's job hunt?"

"Sure, yeah, that'll be fine."

"Thanks. I'm leaving now, so I'll be there in a few."

"Okay. Bye-bye."

"Bye," Alden said, then hung up.

Mark's mother must have been waiting for him, because she opened the door as he reached the stoop. She smiled warmly at him and waved him inside. "Do you want a cup of coffee?" she asked as he entered.

"No, thanks," Alden replied. "I'm fine."

"All of his things are up in his room. A box up there the policeman gave me."

Alden breathed out sharply. For a moment he feared that Mark's mother would think it was a laugh, and it almost was, so confused was Alden about what to feel. His heart sank and compressed, just like it had before, but the pain faded more quickly in her presence. He felt the urge to fidget—he wanted to wring his hands—but he resisted.

"Thanks," he murmured.

Upstairs, Mark's room was nearly as it had been when Alden and Doug had argued in it not long ago. The mattress was still in the same place on the floor, angled lazily away from the wall, but on top of it now was a small cardboard box. Alden peered into it carefully, as if he feared discovering Mark's face inside, angry at him for considering the things upon which Doug had insisted.

Mark's silver cell phone was propped against a corner of the box and Alden lifted it with reverent care. The battery was dead. He looked around and saw the charger on a low bureau where it had always been. He plugged in the phone and turned it on. The menus were easy to navigate and he quickly found Mark's contact list. He scrolled through the alphabetical list until he saw the right name.

"Tom," he whispered. "There you are."

He thought about adding the number to his own contact list, but decided against it. Even if he deleted it later, there was probably a way to pull off the information. Cell phones were really just little computers, and he didn't know how to wipe the memory clean like he did with a desktop. He stared at Tom's phone number and mouthed it several times, committing it to memory. He could write it down on a notepad when he got back to his car.

He went back downstairs and gave his thanks to Mark's mother.

"Are you sure you don't want some coffee?" she asked.

Alden hesitated. She looked tired and she was probably lonely with Mark gone. "Maybe just one cup," he said.

She poured some coffee from an old coffeemaker into a plain stoneware mug with a handle shaped like half of a heart, then set it down on the kitchen table for him. "Thanks," he said as he took it.

"Sugar or cream?" she asked.

"No, this is fine."

"I could never drink it black," she told him. "Mark couldn't, either, but Harry always did."

She had lost her husband, Harry, a few years ago to a heart attack. Alden recalled that it had happened at night, while they were in bed together. It must have been terrible for her, then and now.

"I don't drink a lot of coffee," Alden said. "I've actually never had it any way but black."

"Oh, well, you have to *try* it, honey."

She poured a bit of cream into his coffee and added a few spoonfuls of sugar. He smiled and took a long sip.

"That *is* better," he told her.

She smiled and nodded triumphantly. "There, then."

"So, how've you been?" Alden asked.

"I'm getting along."

"Me and Doug, too."

There was a moment of silence before she said, "I just don't know why he ever got into that stuff. It never made any sense to me. He was always such a straight-laced kid. Teacher's pet and well-liked and all. It just doesn't make sense."

"I know."

"And you," she said, her eyes teary as she regarded him, "I know you tried *so* hard. He talked about you sometimes, you know. Said it was so good to have someone like you there with him, no matter what. And you were. I saw what was happening to him, *my* boy, and you were always there, no matter what. Didn't matter how turned around he got. You were there, Al, and he always knew that."

I'm still there for him, Alden wanted to say, but he remained quiet. He took a big gulp of the coffee and it was too hot for his throat, but he fixed his eyes on the flowery tablecloth. His heart should have ached, he thought. Listening to Mark's mother talk about her late son's admiration for him should have made him hurt. It reminded him of all that he'd lost, but his heart didn't ache. He didn't feel the same pressure, that sense of inevitable implosion that had taken the strength from his legs and made his hands tingle and shake. Instead he felt anger—an indignation about his murdered friend and the woman across the table. He owed Mark more than a few kind thoughts at his grave. He owed Mark's mother more than idle conversation over coffee.

Suddenly it was clear. It was *righteous* indignation. Someone had murdered his friend. Someone had committed a great evil and he was angered by it. It was natural. It was as it was supposed to be. Alden was reminded of his religious education, his time in Catholic schools among nuns and brothers of the faith. He recalled a black-robed man, Brother Arthur, who had taught him about scripture when he was a boy. Was it not God's righteous indignation that had brought destruction to Sodom and Gomorrah? Was it not righteous indignation that drove Jesus to take up a whip of cords to force the money changers from the Temple of Jerusalem? What, then, was wrong with avenging Mark's murder? *If it was murder,* Alden reminded himself. That Mark's death was murder had not yet been determined, but if it was, what was wrong with acting on the anger sure to result?

"I'm sorry," Alden said, "but I have to run."

Mark's mother nodded. "It's okay, Al. Take care."

Alden stood and left the house. Inside his car, he whispered Tom's phone number as he wrote it in a small notebook. Feeling confident in purpose for the first time since Mark's death, Alden started the car.

It was still early when Alden reached the hill that was downtown. He turned and skirted along the bottom of the slope, on the lowest road that was closest to the lake. It had a fair uphill grade itself, and at the top he turned east again, looking for the correct crossroad to take him north. He found it beside a mall's parking garage and soon saw the cemetery where Mark was buried. It passed on his right and he forced himself to stare ahead. He went straight at a fork in the road and took a left at the next intersection.

The city changed here. It was as if crossing a single street had transported him to another town, populated by another people who didn't live quite the same way or to the same standards as the rest of the suburban world. The peeling paint and rusting cars made his mouth feel thick; he licked his lips as though he could taste the crudeness. The north-south cross street ahead made the intersection he wanted. He pulled his car across the oncoming lane and parked near the corner, disobeying the *No Parking Here to Corner* sign. Looking through the passenger side window he could see Tom's home, the single-story apartment house painted white. He let the car idle and set his head against the headrest to wait. He didn't expect any activity this early.

There was a dark blue Japanese sedan on the street in front of the house. Alden noted the make and model on his small pad, along with the time of his observation. He stared for half an hour, and with no activity to keep his attention, he pulled his car away from the curb and turned down the side street to drive by the house. He cruised slowly and examined the properties outside his window. The lot behind the house on the corner was separated from Tom's lot by a low, poorly constructed wooden fence. Then came Tom's place, then the dirt driveway that led to the dirt-and-grass yard behind the apartment house. He took note of the number on Tom's house and wrote it sloppily on his pad of paper. There was a black coupe on the lot, new and plastered with decals, and a red late-model sedan. It appeared that the driveway was shared with house to Tom's right and the red car was angled slightly behind the other house. Either the blue sedan or the black coupe might have belonged to the dealer. It was probably the black coupe, Alden thought, but time and patience would tell him that.

Alden accelerated and drove around the block, heading back toward downtown. He parked on Main Street when he got there, lucky to see an empty space during the morning rush. The previous golden sunlight had been covered by a light layer of gray clouds that promised a shower or two. He got out of the car and tucked the notepad into his back pocket.

The parking space was near pedestrian Church Street, and at the corner of Church and Main stood City Hall. The wide, three-story brick building with white-framed windows and the narrow white clock tower at its top made his shoulders shiver. He had passed it with Doug on the way to eat while Mark had probably been accepting poisoned drugs. The lowest floor was half underground and that was to be Alden's first stop. He trotted up the granite steps to the tall doors and stepped inside with confidence. He didn't see a stairwell nearby and took the elevator to the bottom floor. He followed signs to the town clerk's office and waited patiently at the desk.

"Can I help you?" asked a gray-haired woman.

"Yeah, hi," Alden said. "I'm looking for the Grand List."

"Down the hall. Follow the signs for the Assessor's Office."

"Thanks."

Alden did as he'd been instructed and found a cramped office filled with old filing cabinets and aging computer terminals. A young man with olive skin rose as he entered and asked, "Can I help you?"

"I'm looking for the Grand List."

The man waved him toward another door on the opposite side of the little office. "Through there."

Alden stepped into the other room. It was larger and brighter, but filled with filing cabinets like the adjacent office. On his left he saw several card files with two thick binders on top. He flopped through the pages of one binder, organized by street, and found the listing for Tom's property. Alden frowned. The name listed was *Brown, Catherine*. He should've expected something like this, given that it was likely a rental property. There was no use looking for the property tax information now, as only the owner would be listed there, as well.

What he needed was Tom's last name. He pocketed his notepad and left the office for the hallway. He could get a last name without great difficulty, but that would have to wait. For now, he could go home and take a nap.

Alden drove past the cemetery and into the old neighborhoods just after two in the afternoon. He parked one street over from Tom's house. In his glove compartment he had several pieces of paperwork from previous automotive work. He rifled through them and selected one at random before leaving the car.

He walked slowly, a pen in one hand and the paperwork in the other. He looked up frequently, following cable television lines with his eyes. At the third house he climbed the steps to the porch and squinted as if examining the end of the line, but before he turned he glanced at the brass mailbox that hung by the door. A few pieces of junk mail were inside.

He continued his walk, examining the cable and electrical lines at each house. On the corner he stepped up to a stoop, then crossed the street and continued the procedure. At Tom's house he ascended to the porch where a black iron mailbox hung with its lid open. Alden feinted a few notes on the paperwork in his hands, then removed one of the two copies and stepped in front of the mailbox. With his body shielding his hands, he removed a piece of mail. "Thomas Forant," he mouthed. He replaced the envelope—it looked like a credit card offer—and returned to the sidewalk. He continued his make-believe inspections to the end of the street and around the corner, then returned to his car to write Tom's last name in his notepad.

He checked his watch. There was plenty of time left for a second trip to City Hall.

The same gray-haired woman greeted him at the town clerk's desk. She smiled up at him and asked, "Can I help you?" in the same tone as earlier that morning. Alden wondered how many times she asked that question in a day, then returned her smile warmly.

"I'm looking for voter registration records."

She nodded. "What name?"

"Thomas Forant."

"Date of birth?"

"Sorry," he said, "I don't have that. If there's more than one, I'd like to look at all of them, if that's okay."

She seemed slightly annoyed by that, but walked away from the desk to a large set of filing cabinets. She searched for a few minutes, then returned with a single sheet of paper.

"Do you want a copy of that?" she asked.

Alden looked it over. He had registered with his current address. His date of birth was listed on the form as December 15, 1980. Alden smiled to the clerk and said, "No, thanks." He wrote the date of birth in his notepad and returned the paper.

He left City Hall and returned to his car, parked several streets away in a small garage. Inside, he removed his pistol and its holster from his belt and locked them in the glove compartment. Leaving the weapon made him uneasy, but the only other option would be to return to his house, which was less appealing.

He left the garage and walked around the corner, where the district courthouse was only one building away. He climbed the granite steps of the old, weathered building and pulled open the dull wooden door. The interior looked almost Victorian, which made the boxy walk-through metal detector and X-ray machine seem completely out-of-place. Alden smiled at the gray-shirted deputy at the desk behind the detector and removed his keys, wallet, notepad, and pen from his pockets.

"Your watch, too, please," the deputy said.

Alden complied, setting his items in a plastic bin that was ferried through the X-ray machine on a rubber conveyor belt.

"Step through," the deputy said.

Alden stepped through the detector and an ominous tone sounded. He looked at the deputy in confusion and his heart leapt. For an instant he doubted the memory of leaving the gun in the car. A wave a relief followed and he said, "Oh, duh," and took his cell phone from its plastic clip. He walked back through the detector and sent the phone through the X-ray machine in another bin.

"Step through."

He did so again and the machine was silent.

"Thank you," the deputy said.

Alden collected his things and walked to the chest-high counter to the left. Sunlight was falling through the large windows opposite, reflecting in a blinding glare on a glossy wooden table near the wall that held various forms. He looked away and leaned on the counter.

"How can I help you, sir?" a plump, blonde woman asked.

"I'm looking for civil court records," Alden said.

"Okay. Do you have a docket number?"

"No, just a name and a date of birth. I'm just looking for anything for Thomas Forant. His date of birth is December fifteenth, 1980."

"Let me take a look," she said.

His wait lasted several minutes, due mostly to three telephone calls the woman was forced to take. The two other visible employees were busily shuffling paperwork. When she returned, she shook her head.

"I'm sorry. Nothing."

Alden shrugged. "It was worth a shot." He smiled. "Thanks anyway."

"You're welcome," she replied. "Have a nice day."

"You, too."

Alden left and walked several blocks down the hill toward the lake, then crossed streets toward a much larger and more modern building of brick and white stone that looked like polished granite. Entering the county

courthouse was much the same as entering the district courthouse, but
security was tighter. Several police officers were present, and even after
putting the contents of his pockets, his cell phone, and his watch in the bin,
he set off the metal detector. Had it been his belt buckle?

"Raise your arms, please," a stern, female officer asked. She waved a
handheld metal detector over him, then said, "Turn around, please." Another
sweep and she said, "Thank you," and called the next visitor.

Alden stepped to the end of the conveyor belt and recovered his
items. A deputy behind the machine said, "I'll have to hold on to these," and
jingled Alden's keys. There was a handcuff key on the ring—a memento
from his former career—and it made sense they wouldn't allow those in a
criminal courthouse.

"Yeah," Alden said, "that's fine. Can I get a claim ticket?"

The deputy dropped the keys into a manila envelope and handed
Alden a worn yellow ticket, the same as he might have received for entering
a raffle. He tucked it into his pocket.

"I'm looking for records," Alden said.

"Second floor."

"Thanks."

He took the elevator up and followed plastic signs on the walls. They
led him around a corner and into a long corridor. Windows lined the left side,
letting in the bright sunlight that made the white tile floor almost unbearably
bright. On the right side was a wall of floor-to-ceiling glass, doors held open
on either end. Inside was a long, chest-high counter of dark, polished wood.
In the middle of the counter was the computer terminal for which Alden was
looking.

At the keyboard, he navigated the blue and yellow screens of text
easily. He had become proficient with the system several months previous,
while working with another police officer who had complained constantly
about the antiquated software. It saved clerks the trouble of searching
through the database themselves, and Alden figured that was worth
something.

He searched using Tom's name and date of birth. It would only look
at dockets from Chittenden County, but that would be a good start. The query

returned one hit. It would be several pages of documentation. Alden sent it to the printer and said to no clerk in particular, "I have one case coming through."

A young man at a desk on the other side of the counter looked at him with mild contempt and replied, "It's ten cents per page."

"That's fine."

The young clerk labored his way to the printer and put the documents in order. It came to eleven pages. Alden paid with two dollars and told the clerk to keep the change, then collected his keys and left the courthouse with the loose pages in hand.

He walked swiftly back to the parking garage, and after returning his holstered pistol to his waistband, looked over the court case. It had happened in 2005. Tom had been hosting a party that had aggravated a few neighbors, and the resulting noise complaint had escalated to a charge of disorderly conduct. Tom had been drunk and verbally abusive to the responding police officers. A citation had been issued and Tom had paid the fine without further complaint.

Alden frowned. He had hoped for something more serious, particularly a drug charge. Still, the absence of information told him something. It meant that Tom was careful with his drugs and the way he did business. He wasn't foolish, or if he was, he had been exceptionally lucky.

Alden set the court paperwork on the passenger seat and started the car. He had other court documents sitting on his desk at home. He would spend the evening with those, then turn in at a reasonable time, if possible.

Tomorrow would be a different kind of day.

Alden's cell phone rang in the early evening. It was Doug.

"Hello?" Alden answered.

"Hey, I'm on my way over."

"Okay, good. See you in a few."

Alden hung up the phone and set it on the coffee table next to the stack of court cases he'd printed that morning. The "technical manual" was beside them. Alden picked it up and flipped through the pages until he found the list of materials needed to build an improvised suppressor. He scanned the page, then set a pad of paper in his lap. The categorized first page was still mostly blank. He flipped it over and started on a fresh sheet.

He transcribed the list of materials from the book and tore the page from the pad. He sighed and yawned, then set everything on the coffee table and stood. He meandered his way to the kitchen and looked through the window. The sky was covered by a monochrome layer of silver-gray clouds. He took a bowl from the cupboard and mixed cereal and milk, then ate it slowly while he waited for Doug to arrive.

When the bell rang and Alden opened the door, Doug's face was tense. Alden shut the door and led the way to the living room. Doug sat on the couch and looked over the papers. "What's all this?" he asked.

"Research," Alden replied. "They're all court cases that ended in conviction for someone who decided to do what we're thinking about doing. Seemed like a good idea to know their mistakes."

"Okay," Doug nodded, "good. How are we going to do this?"

Alden shrugged. "I figure we need a way to get inside, but that shouldn't be very hard. We can probably just make an offer to buy drugs, but I'm not sure about that yet. I need to watch the house for a while and see how it all works. I'm going to start that tomorrow."

"Okay."

"Once we're inside," Alden said, "I'll talk to him. We'll see if we can get him to admit to killing Mark."

"And what if he doesn't?" Doug asked.

"We leave."

Doug frowned. "Fuck that! This guy killed Mark."

"We think he did."

"What?" Doug sat back and crossed his arms. "I thought we were ready to go with this. I thought you were ready to go. You said we were on."

"We are, but we have to know for sure. I won't do anything unless I know for sure. Maybe you can live with murdering him without knowing, but I can't. I won't. No way."

"Okay, well, what if he says he did it?"

"That *is* the question," Alden said in a heavy tone. "Do you really think you can do this?"

"Yeah, I do."

Alden nodded. "Okay, then we're going to need a few things. First, do you still have that old Colt your dad gave you?"

Doug looked confused. "Colt? The Huntsman?"

"Yeah."

"Yeah, I have it. Why?"

"Tell me the story behind it again."

Doug looked at the carpet. "He picked it up from some guy he worked with when I was a kid. It was the first pistol I ever shot."

"Where did the guy he bought it from get it?"

"Who knows?"

"We'll need that gun."

"Why? It's just a little .22 plinker."

"We need a gun with a fixed barrel. Plus, nobody we're connected to is recorded in connection with the gun. They haven't made those pistols in a long time. Chances are pretty good that the records aren't even around anymore." Alden waved a hand. "None of that will be an issue if things go the way they should. After we're done, we'll destroy the gun and dispose of the pieces, anyway."

"I've had that gun a long time."

"You were Mark's friend for longer."

That caused a reaction. Doug looked toward the window and his hands twisted together. After a moment's pause, his face flushed and his eyes narrowed.

"Okay," he said. "We'll use it."

"I can build a suppressor for it," Alden said. "If it works, the shots will be very quiet."

He stepped forward, picked up the handwritten list from the coffee table, and handed it to Doug.

"What's this?"

"I need those things to build it," Alden explained. "You should be able to get all of them from local stores. Pick them up tomorrow before work and drop them off in the morning, when you're off."

Doug looked from the list to Alden and asked, "What if someone catches on?"

"Pay cash and buy things at different places," Alden suggested, "but it won't matter. It's screws and fiberglass and PVC and some brake line. I doubt anyone's going to figure it out."

"Okay."

"And stop shaving. Also, we need to talk about clothes."

"Okay."

Alden sat down on the couch next to Doug and said, "We need something like coveralls, but those might stand out. I was thinking about some light sweatshirts to wear over them, so they don't look like coveralls at all, just sweatshirts and pants, you know?"

"Okay, that sounds good."

Alden picked up the pad of paper and added coveralls and sweatshirts to the categorized list. "Can you pick those things up when you're getting the other stuff?"

"Sure," Doug said quietly, his eyes unfocused. He was struggling with the details, Alden thought.

"We'll also need shoes. Cheap ones. Black, probably, and a couple sizes too big. Get whatever you need. Size eleven will work for me. You want me to write this down?"

Doug handed over the list of materials and Alden updated it to match his own, more organized sheet.

"Order some wigs online," Alden said, still writing. "Good ones. Have them shipped overnight if you can."

"When are we going to do this?" Doug asked.

"I don't know yet," Alden told him, "but soon. While you get these things together, I'm going to take a look at Tom and the house. I'll keep you up-to-date on what I find out. Oh, and I'll need the gun when you drop off the rest of the stuff on the list."

"Fuck," Doug said. "We're really going to do this."

Alden looked at him. His face was still flushed, but his eyes were wider now, excited. His lips were tilted in a smirk and he was trying to crack his knuckles, but he'd never been able to do that very well.

"Yeah, well—"

"I can't wait, man. That piece of shit is going to pay for what he did. It's going to be good, man. I can't wait."

"Maybe," Alden said, "if he admits to it."

"He'll admit."

He probably would, Alden thought, but they wouldn't know until it happened. That thought made his hands feel sticky with sweat. Doug was correct. They were really going to do this. It would happen.

"Listen," Alden said. "I found out a little more about the guy today. His name's Tom Forant, he's about our age, and he's careful. He's never been picked up for anything related to drugs, at least not around here. What we're thinking about doing—it's dangerous. It's dangerous because we could get caught and it's dangerous because we could get killed."

"I know," Doug said, "and it's worth it."

"Just get what we need on the supply side. I'll get what we need on the information side, and when it all comes together, we'll make the final decision."

"Okay. I'll call you tomorrow."

Alden showed Doug to the door and said goodbye, then returned to the living room. He looked at his list on the coffee table and used his cell phone to call Doug.

"Yeah?" Doug asked, his voice clear against the background sounds of the road.

"Rent a car," Alden told him. "Rent it through the end of the month, just in case. Get a minivan."

"Okay. Why?"

"We don't want anything connected to us anywhere near that place. Can you drop it off after you get done with work tomorrow? Or the day after, I guess?"

"Sure."

"Okay, good. I'll talk to you tomorrow."

Alden hung up and carried the phone with him while he turned off the lights and went upstairs. It was still light outside, but he felt exhausted and didn't think he would make any more progress until he'd gotten some sleep to clear his mind.

He woke the next morning at first light. After a shower he fixed himself another light breakfast of cereal and turned on the television. He changed it to the Weather Channel and listened while he ate. It was supposed to be cloudy all day, but no rain was expected.

Through the kitchen window he watched the sky. The clouds were low and flat and nearly white. A red sedan backed out of the covered parking and drove away. Something had changed, Alden thought. He felt different. The world seemed less vibrant and there was a disturbing stillness in the house. The previous day had been productive and he'd felt good about that, but hadn't noticed it at the time. Now, thinking back, it was easy to see, but what had been different? It wasn't the productivity alone. He'd been productive as a deputy, or more recently in his job hunt, but yesterday hadn't been like those things.

He rinsed his bowl and set it on the dish rack. The previous day had brought with it a feeling of competence and accomplishment, but that didn't explain it. It wasn't the addition of a feeling, Alden thought, it was the absence of one. That made sense, and with a sudden, heavy thump in his mind he understood. His heart twisted in a slow, mild ache. It had been a lack of loneliness—the realization brought with it an amplification of the isolation. How long had he been alone? Months now. Almost a year. It had been a long time since he'd felt any strong affection, but yesterday had eclipsed it, or perhaps rendered it insignificant. His task was bigger than that and more important, but now, with the new day, the task seemed distant.

It wasn't distant, was it? He was going to leave the house and gather more information—useful information. He was going to get the items on the list from Doug and he was going to build a suppressor. Why did he feel lonely now, when just yesterday he'd felt so strong?

He adjusted the holstered pistol behind his right hip and took up his keys. He'd have all day to think it through.

Alden drove around the block and approached Tom's house from the opposite end of the street. Halfway along he pulled over to the other side of the street and stopped by the curb. It seemed far enough away to avoid looking suspicious, but close enough that he could easily observe the stoop and front door. He turned off the engine, but kept the radio on and cracked the driver's side window slightly. The sight of Tom's house proved to be the cure for his earlier emotional malaise. His heart skipped and he felt a shot of adrenaline rush through his veins, washing away the vague dullness of the morning. He took the notepad from the console and set it in his lap, then sat back and slid a little lower in his seat.

It was just after eight o'clock on a Tuesday morning and Alden didn't expect much activity. Drug dealers didn't have to get up very early, did they? He was surprised and intrigued, therefore, when he saw the front door open shortly before nine o'clock.

Was that him? The man stepping outside was shorter than average, maybe five and a half feet, with enough fat around his waist to present a soft, dumpy look. He wore khaki slacks and an untucked, unbuttoned blue shirt over a white t-shirt. Even from this distance, Alden could see that his face was wide, pasty, and pear-shaped with full jowls. His dark hair was cut very short and was clearly receding. He stepped down to the sidewalk and walked around the side of the house toward the back lot. He moved listlessly and stuck his head out, which made Alden think of a lesser primate, like an ape or an orangutan.

Tom walked out-of-view and Alden started his car. He put his foot on the brake pedal and shifted into drive. His hands were shaking when he gripped the wheel. The black coupe covered with decals drove out of the lot and turned away. Alden waited until the car made a left-hand turn before he pulled away from the curb.

"Here we go," he whispered to himself. The quiet words were followed by a quiet thought. *Don't fuck up.*

Alden stopped the car at the end of Tom's street. Looking left, he saw Tom turn right and head toward downtown. Alden followed at a distance. There was very little traffic in the neighborhood, but more cars began to clutter up the streets as they approached the taller buildings and he was forced to get closer.

Tom turned at Main Street, accelerating up the hill and away from the city. Alden followed, separated from the coupe by two other cars. The hill leveled out near the university, then sloped downward slightly past a strip mall and the onramps for the Interstate. Tom drove straight, then changed lanes in preparation for a right hand turn. Alden followed, now only separated from the coupe by a single green pickup truck.

The lane curved away from the others, putting them on a less congested road. Tom stayed in the far right lane, then followed a narrow drive to the right just before the drive-up ATM of a small bank. Over the line of trees next to the curb, Alden could see the top of the four-level parking garage for the state's largest mall.

Tom drove into the garage and Alden followed, slowing to increase the distance. Most of the parking spaces were empty. The coupe circled to the right and went to the far corner near the building to park. Alden drove past the spot and around the other side of the garage, where he would be out-of-sight behind the ramp. He parked near the exit, turned off the car, and got out.

Walking quickly around the corner and toward the black coupe, he saw Tom disappear behind the stairwell in the corner of the garage. That seemed odd. There was a vestibule that led to the mall halfway between Alden and the coupe, but Tom had been walking away, toward a corner. The sound of a door opening and slamming shut echoed through the garage. Alden saw the source when came around the stairwell. A metal door was set into the corner, rust seeping from its hinges.

Alden paused. He didn't really have a choice, did he? With a deep breath, Alden turned the latch and opened the door. Before him was a long, narrow hallway. The floor was concrete and there was no ceiling, just the metal structure high above from which florescent lights and heating units hung. Tom was standing halfway down the hall, leaning against the wall opposite one of many doors without handles.

Alden walked forward, keeping his eyes on the floor. There was another door with a crash bar at the far end of the hallway and he headed for it. A glance ahead showed him that Tom was watching him, but there was no interest in his eyes. The door in front of Tom opened, apparently pushed by someone on the other side, and he entered. Alden forced another deep breath and slowed his pace. A small black sign above the door showed the name of an electronics store.

At the end of the hall, Alden pushed his way through the door with the crash bar and found himself inside the mall, just outside of a large department store whose metal gate hadn't yet been lifted. Checking his watch, he saw that he had twenty minutes before the stores were scheduled to open. He sat on a bench and waited.

When the department store's gate rattled upward, Alden walked into the main corridor and turned left toward the electronics store. Tom was inside, his shirt buttoned and a black nametag on his chest. Alden debated wandering through the store, but decided against it and kept walking in the corridor.

He felt foolish. He should've expected that Tom would have a regular job. Why wouldn't he? He was a small-time drug dealer in a college town in the summertime. You couldn't make a living on that, could you? Things suddenly seemed more complicated. Retail hours were flexible, weren't they? Tom's schedule would probably change from week to week and his shifts were probably divided between mornings and evenings.

Alden sat on a bench a short way from the electronics store. How would this retail job affect the plan? They would have no guarantee that Tom would be home at any given time on any given day. That part, at least, they would probably have to give over to chance. He had planned on doing it during the day, when most of the homes near Tom's would be empty. Would that still be possible, or would they have to do it at night, when the sounds of an argument or a struggle would be more likely to attract attention?

Shit, Alden thought. Why hadn't he considered this before? That didn't matter. He had to consider it now. He stood with a sigh and walked away from the electronics store. There was nothing to be gained by watching it and Tom would probably be there for hours. He took his phone from its holder and dialed Doug.

"Hey."

"You sound tired," Alden said.

"I just got home from work a couple hours ago. What's up?"

"Just wanted to make sure you had a plan for getting the errands done today."

"Yeah, yeah. I ordered some stuff online last night."

"Good."

"This is going to get pretty expensive."

"I know. I'll cover half."

"Okay. I'll talk to you later. I need some sleep."

"Okay. Bye."

It was almost six o'clock in the evening when Tom left the store and returned to his car. Alden, nearly dozing at the other end of the garage, sat straight at the sight and turned on his car. He followed the coupe out of the garage and back to the street, but Tom turned right instead of left. He wasn't going home yet, it seemed.

It wasn't very difficult, Alden thought, to follow someone. People weren't very observant if they didn't have some reason to be. Tom brought him past this smaller city's high school and turned left. The road, confusingly divided by concrete slabs and orange traffic barrels, dipped and rose. Near the top of the hill, the coupe's left turn signal began to flash and Alden frowned. The turn would take him into a complex of condos obscured from view by a thick tree line. Alden turned on his right turn signal and the two cars diverged.

Andrea lived in that complex. Alden's jaw clenched as he turned his car around and pulled over to the side of the road. *That bitch.* How long would Tom stay? Would he stay the night? *That bitch.*

. . .

Tom's coupe appeared at the condo complex's exit less than an hour later and Alden pulled away from the curb. *A quickie?* He narrowed his eyes at the little sports car and began the pursuit again. Tom went home.

Alden drove around the block and stopped at the corner, but he didn't see Tom. He was probably inside already. With his hands shaking again, Alden turned off the car and tried to settle back into the seat to think.

Doug would be by with the things he needed in the morning. Hopefully he'd have rented the minivan, too. Until they acted, the days would be somewhat routine. Alden would keep watching Tom when he could, and he'd build the suppressor and work out some kind of plan. It would have to be flexible and that worried him. This wasn't a matter for improvisation, but they'd have to rely on it somewhat. Doug would have to be kept informed, and before they took action he'd have to be instructed. His temper could be a hazard.

What else? They'd need a new set of license plates for the rental car, but an hour or two in a couple of neighborhoods would probably result in a set of New York or New Hampshire tags. They'd need alibis. That might prove difficult. They could always claim to have been with each other, but if anyone investigating suspected that more than one person had been with Tom in the house, that wouldn't be very helpful. He'd have to spend some time thinking about that.

Alden sighed. Fatigue was pulling at the back of his eyelids, but movement at the other end of the street made him sit up straight. An old, white car turned the corner, driving too slowly to be passing by. It almost stopped in the street, then pulled into the dirt driveway beside Tom's house. Alden took up his notepad and noted the time and the car's description.

A tall, lanky figure climbed out of the driver's side. He was wearing an oversized t-shirt and shorts that reached nearly to his ankles. He looked young, but that might have been due to the clothes. Alden jotted down the description, then said to himself, "I'll call you Neil." The nickname seemed to fit. He wrote it below the description for reference in case the same guy showed up again.

Neil jogged onto the stoop and knocked on Tom's door. Tom answered it quickly and Neil went inside. Alden leaned back into the car seat, prepared for more waiting, but Tom's door opened again less than a minute later. Neil jogged back to his car and drove away.

Alden noted the time and set his notepad down in the console. He could see it in his mind. Knocking on the door. Claiming they wanted to buy drugs. Entering the house. Alden wondered what it would feel like to step over that threshold. He imagined it would be like stepping through a thick sheet of something fluid and aggressive and resistant.

That one step would change everything.

IV

The Weather Channel was on television. The meteorologist was predicting a clear, hot day interrupted by afternoon storms. The patch of sky visible through the living room window was a fine, sharp blue. The air conditioner was on, the compressor growling as it sucked in warm air and regurgitated a breeze that felt like it should have carried snowflakes. Alden didn't like the low temperature, but it kept him from sweating as he worked.

Doug was resting on a brown vinyl ottoman and rubbing his bare forearms. He watched Alden's progress silently. The coffee table was covered by thick layers of newspaper and strewn with PVC pipe, lengths of brake line, razor blades, fiberglass matting, and various other supplies that had been on Alden's list for Doug to purchase. Behind the table, sitting on the couch, was Alden with the pistol.

The old Colt Huntsman was the first pistol Doug had ever fired. His father had bought it from someone at work more than a decade ago. The dark blue of the steel had worn away over the years and the wooden grips were scratched and nicked. The end of the fixed barrel—including the tall front sight—was hidden now by the improvised suppressor.

The device was almost finished. Alden's first attempt had failed and sat at the edge of the coffee table—a six-inch piece of PVC pipe with brake line in the middle covered with messy fiberglass resin. He had allowed it to cool too much and he'd been too slow with his work. This time he'd been faster and he had mixed the resin at a much higher temperature. The pipe and brake line were already securely attached to the barrel of the pistol. Now he was rolling steel wool into long, thin strips and packing it tightly into the pipe around the perforated brake line. A few minutes later, he took the cap for the PVC pipe from the table and secured it to the end of the construction with screws.

"There," he said. "That should do it."

"Really?" Doug asked. "That'll work?"

"Hopefully. Can I bring it by your place tomorrow, or will Tiffany be around?"

"She's working until five."

"Good. That's plenty of time."

"It looks pretty ugly."

Alden flipped the pistol over in his hand. The serial number had been on the frame, making it impossible to drill out. Instead, Alden had used an engraver to place several other numbers and letters over the top of the real ones before grinding it all away. It was certainly ugly, but Alden shrugged and said, "Doesn't really matter. I was planning on painting the suppressor, anyway, but we may not even need it."

"You can't even see the sight. And I'm pretty fuckin' sure we're going to need it. Come on."

"I'll mark the back of the suppressor when I figure out the point-of-aim. It doesn't have to be good for more than fifteen feet or so."

Doug stood and walked to the air conditioner. "Can I turn this thing off or what?"

Alden shrugged and Doug flipped the switch.

"So?" Doug said.

"So," Alden replied, "we need to go over this thing. In detail."

Doug nodded and took his former seat on the ottoman. "Okay. Still planning on Sunday?"

"Yeah. I've been watching him for three days. I'll go back again tonight, but I'm pretty sure I'll just see the same things." Alden set the gun down on the coffee table and put his elbows on his knees. "It definitely looks like he's dealing out of his house, so that's good for us. It gives us a way inside, but the timing is going to be tricky."

"Why?"

"He works at the mall. Sometimes day shifts and sometimes evening shifts, so there's no guarantee he'll be home when we want him to be. We'll have to play that by ear. I thought about doing it at night, but the afternoon will be better. We'll have to hope he's there in the afternoon."

"I'd rather do it at night."

Alden shook his head. "People are home at night. If we do it in the afternoon, most of them should be at work."

"Okay."

"Here's how I see it right now," Alden said. "First, we wear the new clothes and the latex gloves. Those gloves *will not* come off until we're done and out of there. We'll go just after noon with the van and make a pass to make sure his car is there. We should park a few streets over and walk. The coveralls and sweatshirts will be okay. A little heavy for the weather, but it's the best we can do.

"The first problem will probably be at the door. Hands in our pockets so he can't see the gloves. We can say we want to buy drugs, but Tom's never seen us before, so he might be suspicious. I figure we can tell him that we're throwing a party and need a lot. That might tempt him. We can probably say that Mark told us that he was good. If that doesn't work, we might be able to shove him inside and do it the hard way."

"I like that idea better," Doug said.

"I'd rather get inside quietly. Once we're in, we'll talk to him. That's it. Just talk." Alden paused to emphasize his last two words. "We'll see where we get. We can escalate if he gets violent, but he seems like a pretty low-key guy. If he admits, well, we'll go from there, I guess."

"You mean we'll pop his ass."

"Yeah, well, I think it's more important to know what we'll do if he doesn't admit to anything."

"Pop him anyway. Come on, you know he did this!"

Alden raised a finger. "If we've only asked questions and he doesn't admit, we haven't done anything wrong. We can deny that we requested drugs and we haven't broken any laws. I don't think we've broken any at that point. We can walk away and there's nothing he can do."

"And if he admits it?"

"If he did it," Alden said, "and if we go through with this, we'll have work to do. We need to have steps planned out. We both need to know them by heart so we don't forget anything under stress. First step is going to be picking up the casings from the rounds we fired. When that's done, we need to find whatever money and drugs he has on him and in his place. We can flush the drugs and take the cash, maybe mess up the place a little and make it look like a robbery gone bad. Step three is getting back to the van and leaving the area. While we're doing that, we'll disassemble the pistol and file down the barrel, the feed ramp, the extractor, and the firing pin. Then we'll hit the Interstate and drop the little pieces of the gun every few miles. When we just have the frame and barrel left, we'll stop and bury it way off the road somewhere. Even if someone finds it and somehow connects it to Tom, the ballistics won't match."

Doug was nodding and smiling. "Awesome."

Alden motioned to the door to his office. "I grabbed some New Hampshire plates yesterday. We'll have to change those and wipe down the van before we return it. We can ditch the clothes in a dumpster just about anywhere, as long as it's far enough from Tom's place. The gloves can go at that point, too, as long as we're careful about what we touch and wipe down the van when we get back to the rental place, like I said."

"Then it's done."

"No," Alden said. "We both go home and have a shave and a shower. I'll call you an hour or so later and we'll meet at the bar that night. We'll have a drink or two and chat. We *will not* talk about Tom. Not on the phone and not at the bar. Just regular talk. If someone ends up connecting us to Tom, it shouldn't seem very likely that two first-time murders had a casual night out at the bar like every other week."

"Okay."

"And we need to have our stories straight. There's really no way we can have good alibis without saying we were with each other, but we can come close. If you work the overnight on Saturday, it makes it seem more routine. I have an online job application ready. I'll submit it as soon as I get back home. I have records of my old applications, so that's routine for me."

"Easy."

"The details aren't," Alden said. "You'll need to make sure your cell phone is at home while we're with Tom. You'll need to remember to check if it rang. If you're questioned and you say you were sleeping—like you should've been after work—a phone call you don't mention could break your story apart. Anything like that. You have to remember everything and be ready to explain it."

Doug took a deep breath. His smile was gone. "Okay."

"This is dangerous," Alden said, standing. "This is the most dangerous thing you or I have ever done."

"I know."

"Are you sure about it?"

Doug stood and stared into Alden's eyes. "Yeah, I'm sure."

Alden nodded. "I'll drive the van to your house on Sunday. We'll leave your car there and mine will be here."

"Okay."

"I'll stop by your place tomorrow to test the suppressor and we'll go over it again. Then, on Sunday, we'll go over it a few more times before we do it."

Doug nodded, but the motion was barely perceptible.

Several hours later, Alden sat on the couch and stared at the Colt and the ugly white pipe that was supposed to make it quiet. That garish plastic alone could probably put him in prison. Suppressors were covered by federal law, weren't they? His heartbeat increased slightly and he felt sweat begin to gather along his hairline, just a tickle and an itch.

He stood and the back of his shirt stuck to his skin. He pulled it away and turned on the air conditioner again. He lingered for a moment, then went to the kitchen where he took his nearly empty bottle of rum from the cupboard. He unscrewed the cap and held it by the neck, tilting it back and forth and watching the golden liquor swirl. Then he tipped it upside down over the sink and sighed.

Outside, the sky was obscured by gray clouds. In the distance they were darker and more menacing. "What the hell are you doing?" he asked himself. He set down the empty bottle and leaned against the counter. What the hell was he doing? Was this really going to do any good? Mark was dead. What would killing Tom accomplish? It would probably make him anxious and paranoid. Doug would probably end up the same way, despite his bravado. What else? The only other person who even knew about the possibility of Tom's involvement was Mark's mother. She probably wouldn't even know Tom was dead. Why should she care? Nothing had been proven.

What was it going to accomplish? Was it about some cosmic balance? Some universal justice in the triumph of good over evil? Alden smirked. There was something to be said for that, he supposed, but it wasn't worth the kind of risk they were taking. No one would benefit from Tom's death. Nothing would change.

"That's not true," Alden said. That wasn't true at all. He wouldn't benefit and Doug wouldn't benefit, but someone would. Someone would be spared the hell that Mark had been through. The recreational users and the junkies would just go elsewhere, but Tom wouldn't introduce anyone else to his sick world. Other dealers might do it, but not Tom. There was that, and if even one person avoided Mark's fate, by extension that person's family and friends would avoid Alden's fate and that of Mark's mother. That was something. That was change.

He picked up his car keys and went outside. He needed to buy a can of black spray paint.

Alden was ready to leave by eight o'clock the next morning. He left his own pistol behind and tucked the Colt—the suppressor now coated in matte black paint—into the back of his waistband before walking to his car. It was uncomfortable and the length of the suppressor made him feel awkward; he worried that someone would notice the odd bulge behind his back pocket. Sitting in his car was even more uncomfortable and he had to remove the pistol from his waistband and tuck it under the passenger seat. He had considered wearing gloves while handling it at this point, but that wasn't really necessary. If he was caught with it in his possession the gloves would only serve as circumstantial evidence that he had some malicious intent. And he *did* have that, didn't he?

His first stop was a gun store ten minutes away. It was a squat building with a stone façade next to a busy gas station. The small parking lot was rough with frost heaves that made Alden grimace as he parked. Inside, a

musty concrete stairwell led down to the shop in the basement. The space
was utilitarian; the floor and walls were bare concrete and many of the
weapons were displayed in long glass showcases marked with a haze of
scratches. The long guns stood on racks behind the cases, but Alden wasn't
interested in those. He went to a shelving unit in the middle of the room and
looked over the small cardboard boxes of .22 caliber ammunition. He
selected four small boxes of fifty rounds each, the sides of which read *.22
Long Rifle, HP,* and *Subsonic.*

He waited while the thin, short-haired clerk removed a revolver from
a showcase for another customer. While the customer examined the weapon,
the clerk came to the register and asked, "That'll do it?"

Alden nodded. "That's it."

He paid with cash and accepted the receipt, then returned to his car.
Doug's house was almost forty-five minutes away in the foothills of the
Green Mountains. The commercial sprawl of this part of the state gradually
gave way to the deeper, rural character that had persisted for years. The
businesses became sparse and the homes gradually moved apart, becoming
separated by miles of wooded hills. Halfway to Doug's house, Alden rolled
down his window and let the receipt flutter away.

Doug lived on a remote road in a single-story farmhouse at the base
of a long, steep hill. The white paint on the house was old and showing
cracks and the wooden porch was creaky and gray with age. Alden parked
his car behind Doug's maroon SUV and got out.

"Hey," Doug said, appearing on the porch with several folded papers
and a plastic tape dispenser in his hand.

"I figured you'd be sleeping."

"I haven't been very tired lately."

Alden opened his passenger side door and took out the pistol and
ammunition. "Ready to try it?" A car passed by and he lowered the pistol
out-of-sight beside his leg.

"Let's do it."

Doug had constructed a small, short-range shooting berm behind the
house a few years ago. The range was hardly more than twenty feet, but it
had worked well for Alden when he was training for draw shots and fast,

close-range shooting before the academy. An old sawhorse sat in front of the low, earthen mound and a thin wooden frame, like a block letter "A," sat beside it. Doug unfolded one of the targets and taped it to the frame in several places. The paper was off-white with several thick, black circles surrounding a one-inch black dot with an "X" in the center. Doug paced off about fifteen feet and they stood together there.

Alden ejected the magazine from the pistol and tucked the gun into his waistband at the small of his back. He placed the boxes of ammunition on the ground and opened one. The magazine held ten rounds, but he only loaded one in case there was a flaw in the suppressor and something bad happened. When he stood, he removed the pistol from his waistband and slid the magazine into place.

Alden chambered the gun by cupping his left hand over the top of the small slide and racking it quickly rearward. Doug took a step back and waited. Alden brought the gun on target—or as close as he could manage without a front sight. The diameter of the suppressor obscured the paper. He lowered the gun, then raised it several times, trying to picture where the "X" should be. He squinted and pressed the trigger smoothly backward.

The pistol fired properly, but Alden wasn't sure and kept it pointed at the target for several seconds, treating it as if the round hadn't gone off. After a moment he lowered the weapon and looked at Doug.

"That fired, right?"

Doug's eyes were wide and he was grinning stupidly. "Fuck yeah, it did. Did you hear that? That was awesome."

"Not much louder than a pellet gun," Alden said.

"It just sounded like air."

He looked at the target. The tiny hole in the paper was four or five inches below the center and slightly to the left. "Not too bad," he said.

"For a girl," Doug chided.

Alden's stomach felt buoyant and he loaded the magazine with five more rounds, then asked, "Do you have any Wite-Out?"

"I think so," Doug said. He went inside the house and returned a minute later with a small bottle of generic correction fluid.

Alden took the brush and dabbed a small white dot on the back of the suppressor where he thought the top of the front sight would be. That done, he took aim at the paper again, leveling the dot in the notch of the rear sight and covering what he expected was the center of the paper. He fired one round, then looked. The hole was closer to the "X" and nearly on the center line, but still low. Alden rubbed away the dot and made another just above where it had been. He took aim and fired again. It was amazing how quiet the shot sounded. It was hardly more than a short burst of compressed air. The third hole was higher, just on the line below the "X" and slightly to the left. Alden figured the horizontal deviation was his problem and rubbed away the dot, placing the next one slightly higher. Had he left the second dot, the two would have been touching.

He took aim and fired a third time, taking care to press straight back on the trigger in one smooth motion. Before he could look, Doug exclaimed, "Yes!" The hole was nearly touching the "X." Alden brought the gun up and fired again. The fourth hole was half an inch from the third.

"A few more," Alden said, "and we'll head inside to go over things again."

It was surreal, Alden thought. The pistol was sitting on the coffee table. He had thrown away the newspapers and the excess materials in a dumpster a few miles away. Now he sat watching television. It was supposed to be cloudy and relatively cool the next day.

He looked at the pistol. Yes, it was surreal, he thought, that in less than twenty-four hours it would probably have killed a man. Well, maybe it would, maybe it wouldn't. Drugs from Tom had definitely killed Mark, but it could've been a mistake. Maybe Tom didn't know he was selling something that was cut the way that batch had been. Maybe, but probably not. Carfentanil wasn't used that way. He was just having last minute jitters.

He'd killed a man before. He'd shot him twice, both bullets cutting through the same lung. The bastard had died before the paramedics had arrived. Despite the pathetic, sucking breaths and the wet, bloody coughs,

Alden hadn't felt an inclination to do anything but watch. He hadn't even wanted to finish it. That asshole had deserved to suffer.

If Tom had knowingly given that tainted heroin to Mark, wasn't he the same as that poor, fat, drunk idiot? Alden grunted and stood. He went to the bathroom, but didn't touch the light switch. He looked at his face, one half illuminated by the yellow-white light from the hallway, the other half covered by shadow. He turned his head back and forth, watching the light advance and retreat across his features. His heart faltered and twisted in a brutal ache that made him grip the edges of the sink.

He panted at the floor, then looked up at his reflection again. A sheen of sweat had gathered at his hairline. "What do you have to lose?" he asked himself with a sneer. "Your career is gone. You're alone. You only have one friend left, for Christ's sake." He swallowed past a tight lump in his throat and offered the mirror a bitter snort. "There's nothing left for you here."

He thought of the night he'd met with Tranis. He thought of Andrea and they way she'd held Tom. The way Tom's hands had moved over her back. The familiarity. The confidence.

Alden opened the medicine cabinet and took an over-the-counter sleeping pill from its package. He wouldn't be able to sleep without it tonight, and he would need to be rested and alert the next day.

The morning was cool and cloudy. As he walked to a nearby side street, Alden watched the shades of gray slide silently overhead. He'd never made enough time for himself. It was always work or chores or errands. There were always projects around the house or friends in need.

Like Mark. He had been in need, but Alden hadn't been able to help him. Nothing had worked. Every attempt had ended in failure.

"This won't," Alden told himself.

The keys to the minivan were in his pocket. He hadn't thought of where he would carry the suppressed pistol while wearing coveralls, so he'd left them behind in favor of work pants and a dark green hooded sweatshirt. The weapon was tucked uncomfortably into his waistband, but he was more distracted by the odd feeling of his oversized shoes.

He carried a duffel bag in each latex-gloved hand. One held a change
of clothes, several pairs of latex gloves, pliers, a screwdriver, a rat-tail file, a
pair of handcuffs, and a few pieces of cloth. The other bag held a pair of
coveralls and a pair of shoes for Doug. He'd removed the handcuff key from
his keychain and attached it to the rental's ring.

The champagne-colored minivan was parked a block away. The New
Hampshire license plates were already attached; the rental plates were hidden
under the passenger seat.

Alden opened the passenger side door and put the bags on the floor.
He checked his pockets for his folding knife. He'd decided it was probably a
good idea to have one ready. He paused for a moment, pondering what he'd
forgotten. Unable to think of anything, he climbed into the minivan, stowed
the pistol under the seat, and started the engine.

He drove carefully, keeping his speed a few miles per hour under the
limit. He didn't turn right on red lights. It took longer than usual for him to
get to Doug's house, but he'd planned for that. They met outside, but Alden
motioned toward the house and said, "Let's go over things again."

Doug's bedroom was at the end of a long, creaky hallway. Alden
talked while Doug put on the coveralls and packed a new set of clothes.
When they had reviewed the plan twice, Alden asked, "You sure you have all
of that?"

"I'm sure."

"Do you need to use the bathroom?"

"Probably should."

Doug walked into the hallway and Alden paced in the bedroom. He
ran his hands over his beard and scratched at his neck. Doug's bed was
messy and there was a bunch of clothes on the floor by the closet. Alden
kicked a stray sock back onto the pile and leaned against the frame of the
closet's doorway. Doug's stainless pistol was sitting on a high shelf.

"Hey," Alden said loudly, "you ever get your 1911 fixed?"

The toilet flushed and Doug came back to the bedroom. "Yeah," he
said. "Something about the feed ramp."

Alden shrugged. "Good. Ready?"

Doug nodded as he pulled on a pair of gloves and they went outside to the minivan. Alden's heart was already beating fast and he could feel the adrenaline in his veins, making his muscles ache for movement. Doug seemed calmer. He sat mostly still, although once in a while he would tap out some obscure rhythm on the console. His face was slack and red. He kept his eyes on the road ahead, but they seemed unfocused.

The drive into the city took more than an hour. As they passed the graveyard, Alden said, "Here we go. Head's up."

Doug straightened in his seat. He was sweating and his breathing was starting to become more rapid.

A moment later they were on Tom's street. "That's the house," Alden said, indicating with a pointed finger below the window. He kept the minivan's speed constant and didn't turn his head as they passed, but Doug looked over and kept looking.

"The car's there," Doug said.

Alden parked on the next block. He turned off the minivan and tucked the keys into his pocket, then looked at Doug.

"Let's do this," Doug said.

"Stick to the plan," Alden said, reaching under the seat. "No deviation. Got it?"

"Yeah, got it."

Alden tucked the pistol into the back of his waistband. As he stepped out of the minivan he made sure his sweatshirt was covering the weapon's grip. Doug hadn't been able to get wigs and hats probably would've been a good idea, but it was too late for that now. He took the handcuffs from his bag and put them in his back pocket. They started toward Tom's street quickly, but Alden slowed the pace.

His legs felt weak and insubstantial and he had to work hard to keep his breathing steady. His eyes wanted to stay on the sidewalk, but he forced them to keep moving, looking for witnesses or signs of trouble. He saw none. It was just after noon, but the weather looked bad. No one was outside. They turned the corner onto Tom's street. Alden felt another rush of adrenaline and looked at Doug, whose face was now splotchy.

"Stay cool," Alden said breathlessly. "I'll do the talking."

Doug only nodded.

They reached Tom's stoop. Alden paused for an instant, then climbed the chipped concrete steps. He took a deep breath at the door and knocked three times. His face felt hot and he could feel sweat sliding away from his armpits and down his sides.

The lock turned and the deadbolt clunked aside. The door opened and Tom filled the space. Alden looked at him and his excitement changed. The hot, heady rush of adrenaline-filled blood went cool. The anxiety turned suddenly to exhilaration as Alden felt himself dropped from a great height into the perfect position.

Here he was, Alden thought. He was looking into that chubby, bespectacled face. He was seeing the pasty skin and yellow teeth of the man who'd murdered his friend. This was Thomas Forant, dressed in jeans and a white t-shirt and enjoying his day off. This was the man who would soon be a corpse.

He didn't know. That was it, Alden realized. Tom had no idea what was about to occur, but Alden knew. He was as close to omniscient as he ever could be. He'd never known this level of control, this kind of superiority, but he was sure he belonged here. This was a moment that most men would never experience. This was the silence before the panther leapt, the tranquil hush before the hawk struck.

"Tom?" Alden asked.

"Who're you?"

"Hey, look," Alden said with a grin, "I need to pick up a few things for tonight."

Tom looked between Alden and Doug, then said, "I don't know what you're talking about. I don't know you."

"Mark recommended you," Alden said, "before he got dumb."

Tom was quiet.

"I've got a party tonight," Alden continued. "I know it's a lot on short notice, but whatever I can get, you know?"

Tom shifted his weight from side to side, then said, "Sorry. I'm not sure I can help you." He started to close the door.

Alden's stomach tickled and flipped. This was the instant! His left hand shot forward, the edge striking Tom's throat and pushing the dealer inside. Alden stepped forward as Tom clutched his neck, gasping. Doug followed and slammed the door shut. Alden reached under his sweatshirt and pulled the pistol from his waistband. His spine shivered as he brought the painted white dot in line with Tom's body.

"Stop!" Alden said fiercely. "Show me your hands!"

Tom had stumbled back against the arm of a floral patterned couch and was looking at Alden with wide eyes.

"Hands!" Alden commanded.

Tom, still coughing, brought his open hands to either side of his face and rasped, "Okay, fuck! Okay!"

Alden used his left hand to take the handcuffs from his pocket and held them out. "Cuff him."

Doug took them and roughly turned Tom around, then locked the restraints over Tom's wrists. Tom yelped and swore.

"Too tight?" Alden asked as Doug moved away.

"Fuck, man!" Tom said as he turned back toward them. His surprise had turned to anger. "What the fuck is this?"

Alden tucked the pistol into his waistband and approached Tom. He leaned close to the dealer's face and paused, then turned him around and searched him, but found nothing.

"Get the hell off me!" Tom said.

Alden grabbed Tom's ear and put his lips next to it. "If you don't shut up, I won't be so nice."

"Fuck you!"

Alden took Tom by the arm, shoved him onto the couch, and took a step back. This was the living room. This was where he'd seen Tom and Andrea the night he'd met with Tranis.

"Windows," Alden said, pointing. Doug quickly shut the curtains, leaving the room lit by dim gray light glowing around the edges of the dingy mauve cloth.

"You're fuckin' dead," Tom spat.

"You're fucking scared shitless," Alden replied in a dull tone, "because you know why we're here." He took the pistol from his waistband again and held it casually at his side. "Why are we here, Tom?"

Tom stared at him.

"It's not a rhetorical question."

Doug stepped beside Alden, then started pacing.

"You don't know what you're doing," Tom said, but his voice was softer and he looked toward the front door.

"Yes, we do," Alden said, "and so do you. You've been a bad guy, Tom. You've hurt people. Some people don't like that."

"People like us, motherfucker," Doug said, glaring.

Alden nodded. "Why am I here, Tom?"

Tom narrowed his eyes and spat. Alden smirked, then started as Doug flew past him toward the couch.

"Hey!" Alden shouted.

Doug shot his fists toward Tom's head, swinging wildly and mostly missing, but a few of the punches landed well. Tom's nose cracked and bled. His teeth were rattled and blood washed over his tongue and sputtered from his lips. Alden tucked the pistol at his back and grabbed Doug's shoulders with both hands.

"Stop!" Alden said. "Stop!"

It took several seconds to pry Doug away. Tom slumped over and fell onto his side on the couch, groaning and whimpering. Alden shoved Doug back with one hand and held up a finger in warning.

"Just fuckin' do it!" Doug said.

Alden squinted at him and gave a quick shake of his head, then turned back to Tom. The dealer was crying. The tears mixed with blood and stained the embroidered flowers on the old couch cushion.

"Look at me, Tom," Alden said. "Look at me."

Tom glanced meekly upward.

"Now look at him." Alden pointed a thumb at Doug. "How many times do you think I'm going to be able to pull him off you? Huh?"

Tom stared. Alden took him by the throat and forced him upright. They looked at each other, Tom's eyes wide and glossy, Alden's wild and eager.

"Why am I here?"

Still no answer. Alden took the pistol in hand again and placed the end of the suppressor against Tom's left knee.

"No!" Tom shouted.

"Finally!" Alden replied. "We're talking. That's good. We need to talk. We'll start at the beginning again. Why am I here?"

Tom was sweating heavily and he smelled sour. He sucked in great breaths and shook his head, then blurted loudly, "It wasn't my idea! I just gave him the bag! Fuck! It wasn't my idea! It's not my fault! Come on, man. Come on, please, it wasn't me."

"You swear?"

"Yeah, Jesus, I swear. I swear."

Alden raised the gun to Tom's throat. "Whose fault is it?"

"Oh, come on, man. They'll fuckin' kill me!"

Alden stood straight and took a step back. He fixed Tom with a look of disbelief and held out the pistol. "They'll kill you? Have you looked around since I sat you on the couch? You do know what's going on, right?"

"Come on, man. Please. *Please!* Don't do this."

While Tom whimpered, Alden looked around the room. Doug was standing by the door to what looked like the kitchen, his shoulder against the wall and look of grim satisfaction on his face. There was a small desk between the two windows with a wooden chair in front of it. Alden grabbed the chair and swung it around to face the couch, then sat.

"Please, man. Don't do this. Don't do this."

Alden let his gun hand rest on his thigh and said, "Listen. Listen, Tom. I'm here to make you go away. As I see it, there are two ways that can happen. One, I can put a bullet in your head." He paused and raised the gun, then set it against his leg again. "Two, you can start talking to me and we can come to another arrangement. Maybe you can disappear some other way, you know?"

Tom was nodding slowly, his eyes distant and confused.

"You need to be honest with me."

More nodding.

"If you lie to me, I'll kill you."

The nodding stopped.

"Do you understand, Tom? You answer my questions and do what I tell you to do, and maybe we can work something out. Understand? Tell me you understand what I'm saying."

"I understand," Tom croaked.

Doug resumed his pacing behind Alden's chair. Alden glanced back at him and winked. Doug smirked and nodded and Alden turned back to Tom. The dealer's face was covered in blood and tears that dripped from his nose and chin while he stared at the dusty brown carpet.

"We'll start with the easy part," Alden said. "What did you give to Mark when he came to talk to you about Andrea?"

Tom was quiet for several seconds, then looked away to his left and said, "I don't know what it was."

"What did Mark think it was?"

Another long pause, and then, "Just some dope."

"But you knew there was more to it, right, Tom?"

Tom's eyes rose and met Alden's.

"Right, Tom?" Alden asked again.

Tom nodded and Alden mirrored the motion, then leaned forward and said, "Good, Tom. Good. This is what we need—this kind of honesty. Relax, Tom. I just need you to keep being honest with me and I think things will be okay."

Tom continued nodding absently, but returned his gaze to the floor.

"When you gave the stuff to Mark," Alden said gently, "did you know what would happen when he used it?"

Tom took a deep, shuddering breath and whispered, "Yeah."

"Before, you said it wasn't your fault. Whose fault was it? I know you gave him the drugs, but whose fault was it that he died?"

Tom shook his head. "They'll fuckin' kill me, man."

Alden stood with such force that the chair skidded backward and toppled. He stepped forward and pushed the end of the suppressor hard into

Tom's forehead, eliciting a scream that sent a spray of blood from the
dealer's lips.

"No!" Tom yelped, "No!"

Alden growled, "Who's at fault?"

Tom screamed, then sobbed, "Pedro! Pedro. Pedro."

"Who's Pedro?"

"I don't know him! He just works for Tips! I don't fuckin' know
him, I swear! I only saw him once!"

Alden stepped back and let Tom catch his breath, then asked, "What
do you mean, he works for tips?"

"Not like money tips. Tips."

"Like a name?"

Tom nodded and starting crying again.

"Who's Tips?"

"He gives me…most of m-my shit."

Alden looked back at Doug, who now was sitting against the edge of
the desk with his arms folded over his chest. His eyes were burning with rage
and he was licking his lips repeatedly. He didn't notice Alden's attention.

"Forget about Tips, Tom," Alden said, picking up the chair and
sitting again. "Why is it Pedro's fault?"

"He g-gave me the shit."

"He gave you what you gave to Mark?"

Tom nodded.

"You don't know him. Why Pedro?"

Tom shrugged and his head swayed helplessly. "He's supposed to be
up here to find some new people for Tips. He gave me the sh-shit when I told
Tips about Mark—the trouble he was making."

"What kind of trouble was he making?"

"He started saying he was going to go to the cops. Shit like that, you
know? I mean, fuck, man."

Alden feinted a sympathetic nod. "Because you were with Andrea?"

"I don't know. I guess so."

"Where's Pedro now?"

Tom's voice broke when he asked, "Why?"

Alden was silent for a few seconds, then said, "You don't get to ask questions, Tom. Where's Pedro now?"

"I don't know him. Please."

"You don't know him, but you know how to get in touch with him, right, Tom? You can get in touch with him."

Tom looked toward the door, but the motion was slow and hopeless. Alden stood and Tom's eyes drifted back to him.

"You're going to get in touch with Pedro for me, Tom."

The dealer shook his head and swallowed blood.

Alden nodded. "Yes, you are. You're going to get in touch with him and set up a meeting. You're going to do it now. When it's done, if you do it right, just like I tell you, I'll let you go."

Tom's head stopped shaking.

"I'll let you go," Alden continued, "and I'll talk with Pedro about this business. If he gave you the drugs, you were just his tool. You were just used. I'm here for the user, but the user isn't here, understand?"

"I can't."

"Why not?"

"They'll kill me."

"Who'll kill you?"

"Tips."

Alden moved the chair back to the desk and met Doug's angry eyes briefly, then moved in front of Tom again.

"In that case," Alden said, "you have a choice to make. Two options. One, you can set up a meeting with Pedro and risk pissing this Tips guy off. Two, I can kill you right now." Alden brought the white dot on the back of the pistol's suppressor in line with Tom's head. "Choose."

Tom recoiled into the couch cushions and squirmed, but Alden insisted, "Choose," and took a half step forward.

"Let me do it," Doug said.

Alden glanced back and replied, "Wait," then turned back to Tom and asked, "Well? Set up a meeting or I give him the gun and let him kill you. He's not as good a shot as I am, Tom. It'll hurt. It'll be bad."

"Okay!" Tom screamed into the arm of the couch. "Fuck! Okay! Okay! I'll call him. I'll fuckin' call him. I'll call him."

"Where's your phone?" Alden asked.

Tom pushed his chin toward the television and Alden saw the silver cell phone on top of it. He picked it up and turned back to Tom. "Is the number in here?"

Tom nodded. Alden scrolled through the list of contacts until he saw the right name. He turned the screen toward Tom and asked, "Is this the one?"

"Yeah."

"Get yourself together. I'm going to call him and you're going to set up a meeting today. Be cool. Act like a professional and I'll treat you like one, got it? If you fuck it up or warn him, I'll let this guy kill you. Got it?"

"Yeah," Tom said to the floor.

Alden pulled up the phone number on the screen and mouthed it silently several times, then pressed the *send* button and held the phone to Tom's ear. He kept the pistol at his side, but in Tom's view, and leaned in close enough to hear the conversation. Doug stepped away from the desk and stooped to listen.

The ringing stopped a nasal voice asked, "What's up?"

"It's Tom."

"I know, what's up?"

Tom squeezed his eyes closed and said, "Listen, uh, I need to pick up some more stuff. Guy's having a party and I don't have enough."

"Enough what?"

"Coke."

"I still have some. How much?"

"A key, maybe."

"This is short notice. He pays up front."

"That's cool."

"When can you be here?"

Alden nearly asked, "Where's here?" but stopped himself. He narrowed his eyes at Tom.

"Not sure," the dealer said, "but not too long."

"Yeah, well, I'll be here for a while," the voice said, "but I'm going out tonight. Don't hold me up."

"Okay," Tom replied.

Alden waited, but the voice didn't sound again. When he looked at the phone's screen, he saw that the call had ended and he put the phone back on top of the television.

"Where are we meeting Pedro?" Alden asked.

"Golden Gate Motel."

"Where's that?"

"Plattsburgh."

Alden paused, surprised. "New York?"

"Yeah, New York, asshole."

"Where in Plattsburgh?"

Tom shook his head, more angry than scared. "On the way in, before you get in town. A little ways from the plant."

Alden nodded. "Okay."

"Let me go," Tom said.

"I will," Alden replied, "but there's one more thing you need to do for me first."

"Fuck you, bitch! You said you'd let me go!"

"Call it your lesser penalty, Tom. Where do you keep your cash?"

"Oh, hell no."

"Okay," Alden said. "My friend is going to have a look around. If he finds the cash before you tell me where it is, I'm going to kill you."

Tom spat and sat up as straight as he could. Doug forcefully pulled the drawers from the desk. He turned them upside down and kicked through the contents as they spilled onto the carpet, but found nothing. Tom watched him, his breath coming faster and his eyes getting wider.

Doug moved to the television and pushed it from its stand. It thudded onto the floor and Doug tipped over the wooden base, finding nothing beneath it. He continued around the room for several minutes, roughly handling Tom's possessions and breaking whatever he could. When he found nothing in the living room, he moved into the hallway and out-of-sight.

Alden listened to the jarring sounds of Doug's search and said to Tom, "He's going to find it eventually, Tom. I'm going to kill you if you don't tell me. Just tell me, Tom."

"Fuck," the dealer spat. "Okay, fine. Fine!"

"Hey," Alden called, "come back in here."

Doug appeared and waited.

"Where's the cash?" Alden asked.

"In my closet," Tom said, "there's a hatch to the attic."

"Check," Alden said to Doug, "then come back."

Doug went back into the hallway. Alden stood in front of Tom, looking down at him. He hefted the pistol and adjusted his grip. His latex-covered trigger finger, held straight against the frame, tapped an erratic beat against the steel.

"Got it," Doug said as he came back into the living room. His hand gripped the black plastic handle of a cheap aluminum toolbox painted red. He set it down on the desk and opened it. It was filled with bundles of cash held together with rubber bands.

Alden stepped close beside him, his back to Tom. He held out the pistol and Doug took it.

"No more than five rounds," Alden whispered. "If he isn't dead, I'll finish it. No more talking. No taunting. Just do it."

Doug looked at the gun in his hand and moved in front of Tom. The dealer looked up at him and his bloody mouthed opened. He shook his head as if convulsing.

"No! You said—no!"

"This is for Mark," Doug said as he brought the pistol in line.

Alden watched him fire the gun. He saw the action work as Doug pulled the trigger, jerking it back with more force than necessary. He watched as the polished brass casings were thrown to the side, noting where each landed, bounced, rolled, and stopped. Doug fired five rounds. The first three entered Tom's chest and stomach. The forth struck him in the throat, off-center and beneath the jaw, an instant before the fifth missed. Sprays of crimson leapt across the living room in time with Tom's racing heart. Alden pushed himself away from the desk and pulled Doug away from the couch as Tom writhed and gasped and choked.

They stumbled into the kitchen and watched through the doorway. They winced and ducked whenever Tom's movements sent the pulsing stream of lifeblood their way. The dealer struggled against the handcuffs and fell onto his side, then rolled from the couch to the floor. Spasms of terrified motion accompanied his coughs as blood spurted from his lips.

Alden suddenly felt sweat building on his upper lip and his excited sense of power reverted to balmy anxiety. His stomach twisted and hardened around a single, burning point.

Tom's writhing slowed. The blood continued to spray from the wound in his throat. The carpet was lined with long, thin stains and the baseboard showed several speckles and splashes of crimson in the dim light. Eventually, after what seemed like many slow minutes, Tom rolled over, halfway between being on his side and prone. The blood came more slowly from the wound, the volume lessening to little more than a trickle. His eyes were open—glassy and dark—and fixed on the wall beside the doorway to the kitchen. His breathing had stopped. His heart had stopped.

Alden took the pistol from Doug, who hardly noticed, and stepped carefully into the living room, trying to avoid the blood on the carpet. He moved beside Tom's body and brought the white dot on the suppressor in line with Tom's head, then fired a single shot. It left a small, dark hole above the dealer's ear, along his hairline.

"It's done," he said.

"Yeah," Doug said quietly. Then, after a few seconds, he said more forcefully, "Fuck yeah."

Alden tucked the pistol into his waistband, then picked up the six brass casings and put them in his pocket while Doug stood in the kitchen, watching. There was blood on the side of the toolbox.

"Get a towel or something to wipe this off," Alden said.

Doug was still for a moment, then nodded and went into the kitchen for a dish rag. He carried it slowly through the living room and handed it to Alden, who used it to clean the toolbox. When it looked clean, he removed the handcuffs from the corpse's wrists and wiped them clean, too.

"Go to the bathroom," Alden said, "and wash the blood off your gloves. Keep them on."

Doug went into the hallway and Alden put his hands on the desk as adrenaline flooded his veins. His heart pounded so hard that it made his head swim and he felt the burning point in his gut explode. Blistering panic made his whole body quiver with tension. His eyes jumped from the cash to the curtains and his ears burned. Was that a siren? He strained to hear and growled with annoyance at the muted sound of running water coming from the hallway.

No, there was no siren. There was no siren and there would be no siren. Not yet. Not until someone found the body. He ground his teeth together until the pain in his jaw forced him to stop. He shouldn't have let Doug do the shooting. The place was a mess, but that didn't matter. Hiding the body wouldn't matter anyway. It would look like a robbery even without a body and someone would call the police about that. It didn't matter.

Doug came back into the living room and Alden saw that the same feelings must have been running through him. His hands were shaking uncontrollably and he leaned against the wall, breathing heavily.

"Okay," Alden said, as much for himself as Doug. "We're okay. It's done. We have to calm down and keep thinking."

He folded the blood stains on the dish rag to the inside and used it to wipe down as much of the inside of the toolbox as he could without removing the cash. There was blood on the top of the desk and he didn't want to get any on the money. He shut the lid and flipped down the clasps.

"We're going to leave," Alden said. "We're going to walk out that door and walk to the minivan. We aren't going to run or walk fast. We're just going to walk. Turn around."

Doug did and Alden said, "I don't see any blood. What about me?"

He turned in a circle and Doug said, "Nothing."

"Come to the door," Alden said.

They stood there and Alden lifted each of his legs. He used the dish rag to wipe the bottom of his shoes as best he could, then handed it to Doug, who did the same. Alden took the rag back and tossed it next to the corpse on the living room floor.

He opened the door and stepped outside. The sky was still gray, but the temperature had risen and the air was thick and moist. Doug shut the door behind them and they descended from the porch to the sidewalk. Alden looked behind them once, but didn't see any blood on the concrete.

"Holy shit," Doug said, a giddy smile slowly drawing a line through his red beard. "Holy shit, we did it."

Alden breathed a smile, but there was no exhilaration behind it. The expression was pushed onto his face by something that ran deeper than his immediate reaction. He could feel it rising up from the pit of his stomach, a smooth, chill expansion that gradually overtook his panic.

"Yeah," he said. "We did it."

"What now?"

The cool satisfaction had displaced all but a sliver of Alden's apprehension by the time they reached the van. He put the toolbox in the back and climbed into the driver's seat, then took the pistol from his waistband and slid it under his seat. His calm smile faded and was replaced by a neutral expression, but his shoulders shuddered involuntarily as euphoric anticipation spilled out from the base of his skull.

"What now?" Doug asked again.

Alden started the minivan and glanced over. "We have something to finish in New York, right?"

Doug paused, then nodded and said in low tones, "Let's go."

V

Alden took the Interstate away from the city, heading north. He checked the speedometer every few seconds, ensuring that his speed was a few miles per hour under the limit. It annoyed him. It seemed like paranoia, but he couldn't stop himself. Any variation in his speed made him nervous and his hands couldn't seem to keep the steering wheel steady enough. Other cars passed him regularly and that annoyed him, too. It was distracting and he needed to think.

Doug was quiet. He watched the scenery through the passenger side window. They had already passed through the suburban and commercial areas north of the city. The view was now dominated by lush green fields and thick woodlands under a patchwork of clouds that obscured all but a few pieces of blue sky.

The air in the car was hot and hard to breathe. Alden turned on the air conditioner and said, "We need to talk through this."

"What?" Doug asked, peeling his eyes away from the window.

"We should be disposing of the pistol," Alden said, "but we're probably going to need it. Unless we decide to let this other guy go."

"No fuckin' way."

Alden nodded. "Then we have to agree on the risks involved. This is getting more dangerous. We can't let it get away from us."

"Okay."

"We're carrying a murder weapon. If we get caught, the ballistics will match the bullets at Tom's place. The bullets in Tom." Alden paused, caught off guard for a moment by his own words. He looked at the four latex gloves bunched in the console and continued, "The gloves will still have blood on them, even though you washed them. They also have our fingerprints on the inside. Those, along with the casings, we can get rid of just about anywhere. We should do it before we cross the lake. There's a gas station near the dock. We can stop there."

Doug looked ahead.

"We're driving to an unfamiliar place on unfamiliar streets. I'm being as careful as I can, but chances are better that we might get pulled over. The plates won't match the van and we'll be screwed."

"Should be change the plates back?" Doug asked.

"If we do that, someone at the hotel could get the plates and they could be traced back to the rental place, then you."

Doug shifted in his seat and flexed his fingers.

"We have a problem with the gun, too."

"What? It was working fine."

"Yeah," Alden said, "it's working fine, but it had eleven rounds— one in the pipe and ten in the mag. You used five rounds and I used one. That only leaves us five rounds. I didn't pack any of the ammunition. I tossed it last night with a bunch of other stuff, so no one could connect the ammo type with something in my house if we got caught."

"Shit. Should we buy more?"

Alden shook his head. "I don't think so. Maybe, but it would just be someone else who might remember us."

"What if we buy it somewhere bigger? Like Wal-Mart or someplace else? Don't they have a Gander Mountain in Plattsburgh?"

"Definitely not. We'll be new faces and they'll have cameras in places like that. Better that we have no contact with anyone."

"Don't they have cameras at the gun shop you use?"

"Yeah, but I'm in there every other week. It's not unusual for me to be buying something there."

"You want to call it off."

Alden shrugged. He should call it off. He should quit now, before he brought on any more risk. He should, he knew, but he wouldn't. The tickle at the base of his skull was still there, subtly spreading indigo shadows of enticing euphoria through his limbs. He was both compelled by memories of his moment of omnipotence and repulsed by the pleasure he had extracted from it. He opened his mouth, then closed it and shrugged again. The conflict in his mind was over. His prurience had won an easy victory. The desire for pleasure outweighed the desire for safety.

"I want to go ahead with it," Alden said.

Half an hour later, with the Interstate behind them, Alden drove the minivan below the speed limit over great, rolling hills toward the lake. The road twisted between high walls of blasted rock and took them through small pockets of country living. The way flattened after a time and the water came into view, dull and gray without the sun. The road straightened and they crossed a long, low bridge built on a bed of rocks that fell away into the lake. A few trucks were stopped on the wide shoulders, their owners on the stones below with fishing lines cast into the choppy water.

Alden checked his speed as they left the bridge and began twisting his way through the island that would connect them to New York. Though the atmosphere was much like the rural one they had just passed through, the houses were closer together and the towns were larger and more developed. The speed limit changed several times over several miles and Alden asked Doug to watch for the signs in case he missed one.

After driving out of a small village and through a short patch of tree-lined fields, Alden saw the gas station ahead at an intersection. He turned on his directional and cut across the oncoming lane into the parking lot. He parked and picked up the bundle of latex gloves, then got out of the car. There were two cars parked at the fuel pumps, but their owners were watching the numbers rise on the displays. Alden crossed the lot to a brown trash can with a metal cigarette tray on the top. He threw out three of the gloves, then used the largest part of the forth to pull the six brass casings from his pocket. He threw the bundle away and returned to the running minivan.

"Okay?" Doug asked.

"Fine," Alden replied.

He drove onto the road that intersected the one he'd just taken. It curved past several farms separated by tracts of woodland, eventually bringing them to another intersection where Alden turned left toward the ferry dock.

The asphalt widened and was divided into multiple lanes. Small white booths sat ahead. The lanes beyond them descended a shallow hill. Two of the booths had green lights glowing dimly at their corners. Alden chose the one on the right side and pulled up slowly. A sign propped up against the white siding displayed in bold text, *MARSEC Level 1*. Alden scratched his eyebrow and rolled down his window. The attendant was an older woman with gray hair, overweight and sweaty.

"Round trip, please," Alden said.

"Sixteen fifty."

Alden fished through his pocket and gave her a twenty dollar bill. She opened a cash drawer and returned his change with two long tickets.

"Second lane," she said as she turned away.

Alden drove down the shallow, curving hill into the second painted lane. The first lane held a long line of cars, but there were only two ahead of them when he stopped. Cars had just begun to leave a ferry at the dock. They drove past the lines of waiting cars until the boat was empty and one of the workers signaled for the first lane to approach. When the lane was clear, she signaled for the few cars in the second lane to drive down. Alden put the van in gear and eased down the slope. The worker stepped over and he handed one of the tickets through the window, then drove onto the ferry and parked amidst the other vehicles.

The ride across the lake was smooth and took a little less than twenty minutes. Alden and Doug were silent, staring at the approaching shoreline dotted with grand houses in the woods above the rocky beach. Might someone be at their window, watching the boat approach? They'd have no idea that it carried two murderers; the thought of such powerful anonymity made Alden smirk. The ferry bumped its way to the dock and the deckhands moved the heavy ropes away from the end of the boat, then began directing the cars ashore. Alden started the minivan and left the ferry, ascending a hill much like the one they'd recently descended and heading toward the city.

"I haven't been here in years," Doug said.

"Me neither," Alden replied. "They changed the roads around, I guess, but we'll get there. I'll find it."

The dock had been recently repaved and the road seemed new and completely unfamiliar to Alden, but most of the cars with Vermont license plates were taking it and he followed them, figuring that they were probably heading where he was heading.

The long, straight avenue into Plattsburgh was four lanes wide. Alden and Doug scanned the road ahead, squinting at the signs. The clouds had drifted away, exposing a sun that made sharp, dark shadows. They had passed a hotel on the right side of the road, but the name hadn't been right.

"Did we miss it?" Doug asked.

They passed a large brick complex on the left, set back slightly from the road. The sign read something about eye care, but it seemed to Alden that it was too big to be a doctor's office near a small city. Just past the complex, rising up from beside the curb, was a square sign that once had been white, but now was discolored a sickly yellow. Red and blue letters announced the Golden Gate Motel.

"There it is," Alden said.

He slowed slightly and drove by it. It was made up of two separate two-story buildings on either side of a parking lot. They were long and narrow and they stretched toward the lake. The place looked run down. Cracked asphalt. Flecks of paint where there once were lines. Stains of rust on the metal posts that supported the second floor. A brick façade on the bottom and faded paint that might have once been taupe above.

He drove past a large industrial plant and turned around at a gas station. As they approached the motel again, Alden asked quietly, "You ready?"

Doug's hands were tapping his knees. "Yeah."

"We're going to have to improvise."

"I know."

"We might get ourselves caught here. Or killed."

"I know."

"You ready for that?"

"Yeah."

Alden took a deep breath. "Can you accept that?"

"Jesus," Doug said, "Shut up and let's go."

Alden braked and pulled into the parking lot. The office seemed to be in the building on the left side. He let the van roll slowly over the cracked lot and looked at the few cars. There were two on the left side, both with Vermont plates. Three more were parked on the right side, one with a Vermont plate, one with a New York plate, and one with a Massachusetts plate. The car from Massachusetts was parked near the back of the lot—a late model Oldsmobile Cutlass 442 painted a pale yellow.

"What is it," Alden asked, "with these guys and their cars?"

Doug didn't answer.

They parked beside the Oldsmobile. Alden reached back and took two pairs of latex gloves from one of the duffel bags and handed a pair to Doug. They pulled the gloves over their hands, then Alden took the pistol from under the seat and tucked it into his waistband at the small of his back. The handcuffs were in the console and Doug took them, then asked, "What room do you think he's in?"

"Plenty of parking. He's right in front of that one."

"Do we just knock?"

"I guess so."

Alden turned off the minivan and looked over. Doug's gloved hands were balled into fists and his face had turned bright red. A drop of sweat had already traced a wet line from his forehead to his cheek. Alden swallowed. He could feel the sweat gathering under his arms and above his lips; his anticipation had turned to anxiety again. There were a lot of unknown factors at play. What was he doing here?

"You sure about this?" Alden asked.

Doug nodded stiffly. "I'm sure."

Alden set his jaw. Why were they here? Tom had claimed that this guy, Pedro, had given him the drugs for Mark. Was that true, or had Tom said anything to get it over with? It was probably true, Alden thought, and that made Pedro part of it, but was he so big a part that they needed to get involved? Did he need to die to do right by Mark?

Had Tom needed to die to do right by Mark? Jesus, Alden thought, Mark hadn't entered his mind the entire time he'd been in Tom's house. The reason why, the one justification, had disappeared. What the hell had happened?

"You okay?" Doug asked.

Alden opened his eyes and shook his head vigorously. "Yeah, I'm okay. Just thinking things through. Ready?"

"As I'll ever be."

They got out of the minivan. The motel's property abutted the lake and they could hear the low waves gurgling over the rocky beach behind the lot. There was a large window next to the door, but the curtains were closed. The number next to the doorframe was 48. Alden rapped his knuckles against the metal door three times. There was a moment of silence, then a voice from the other side.

"Who the hell arc you?"

Alden looked at the peephole and replied, "Tom told us to come over to talk with you."

Another silent moment.

"What are you here for?" the nasal voice asked.

"What you talked about on the phone with Tom."

"Let's see money."

Alden nodded. "In the car. Be right back."

He and Doug walked around the minivan and he opened the back hatch, then the red toolbox. He took a stack of bills and closed the toolbox and the hatch, then went back to the door and knocked again.

"Yeah," the voice said, "I see you."

Alden held the money close to the peephole, keeping his gloved hand low and out-of-sight. After a few seconds he tucked the bills into one of his back pockets. "So?" he asked.

He heard the sound of the deadbolt working and the clatter of the chain on the other side of the door, then it opened. Pedro was short, hardly taller than Tom had been, and thick around the waist. His curly black hair was cut short and flat and he wore a neatly trimmed mustache. Hispanic, Alden thought, but his skin was dark enough to suggest a black parent or grandparent. His hands were empty, but his oversized, baby blue shirt and huge, faded jeans made it impossible to tell if he had a weapon elsewhere.

"Come on in."

Alden and Doug stepped inside. Doug shut the door and Alden looked around the small room. The television was against the right wall playing some made-for-TV movie. The door to the bathroom was near the corner of the far wall, open and displaying the cracked green tile inside. One bed was against the left wall, flanked by nightstands and lamps. A new DVD player in a sealed box was on the bed beside—

Alden's heart, already beating fast, took in a surge of adrenaline and pounded painfully against the inside of his chest. A girl was on the bed. She was dressed in jeans and a white halter top. She was hardly more than a teenager, blonde-haired and blue-eyed and smoking a cigarette. No, Alden thought, smelling the acrid smoke. A joint.

"Who's this?" Alden asked.

Behind him, he heard Doug breathe, "Oh, shit."

Pedro nodded toward the girl and said, "Just a friend of mine."

"Hey," the girl said in a slow, faded voice, "name's Jen. You guys wanna pick up somethin' else while you're here? I got some more of these." She gestured toward the DVD player. "Some portable ones, too, if you want."

"Shut the fuck up, bitch," Pedro said in playful tones. "So, what is it you guys are after?"

"Coke," Alden said, trying hard to avoid looking at the girl.

"How much?"

"Uh," Alden hesitated, "it's a pretty big party. Kilo, maybe."

Pedro chuckled. "Wish my friends threw more parties like you. I can do that. Money first."

Alden took a long, deep breath. What the hell was he supposed to do now? Lure Pedro somewhere else? Outside? No, that would be too public. Stupid idea. Kill the girl? No, she had nothing to do with this. *Kill the girl?* Alden's stomach tightened and he felt briefly nauseous. How had the thought even come into his mind? They could buy the drugs and get out. They could get rid of the cocaine as soon as they left. Dump it into the lake or something, then dispose of the pistol and the rest of the evidence.

"Hey," Pedro said, pulling Alden away from his thoughts. "Money."

"Yeah," Alden said.

He reached for his pocket and his hand felt the grip of the pistol under his sweatshirt. Sweat tingled on his fingertips and made the latex gloves feel slick. Pedro could identify them. He'd find out that Tom had been killed and he would remember this deal. He would probably make the connection. No, he would definitely make the connection. Pedro showed none of Tom's lethargy. Despite his soft figure, his temperament came across clearly. This was business and he was a businessman. He probably thought of it that way. No, they couldn't make the buy and walk away. It had to happen.

"How do we know you even have it?" Alden asked, stalling.

"I guess you'll have to trust me."

Alden put his hand over his back pocket and felt the bundle of cash. Pedro was watching him. His dark eyes were fixed on Alden's hip, as if he was trying to see the money through clothes and flesh. It was a look of anticipation. Seeing that look, Alden felt the same sense of exhilaration wrought of superiority that had struck him when Tom had answered the door. Just like Tom, Pedro had no idea how close he was to death. He had no idea that he was prey. *What about the girl?*

Alden pushed the question away. There was no time to consider it. They couldn't make the deal and walk away. They couldn't let Pedro live. The risks were too great now. It had to happen. It had to happen now.

Doug shifted his weight between his feet as Alden drew the money from his pocket and tossed it onto the bed. Pedro watched it bounce on the comforter and reached for it. Alden took the pistol from his waistband and brought it in line with the dealer's torso. The girl gasped. Pedro looked and his eyes went wide.

"Stop!" Alden barked. "Don't move! Don't move. Put your hands up. Hands up. Let's go. Hands *up!*"

Pedro slowly lifted his hands.

"You, too," Alden said to the girl, who dropped the joint to the floor and complied immediately.

"You don't know what you're doing," Pedro said.

"Turn around," Alden told him. "Face away from me."

"Fuck you, bitch!"

Alden motioned for Doug to move forward. He did, reaching Pedro in a few long steps. He feinted a punch at Pedro's face and the dealer drew his hands together, only to be struck hard in the ribs. He doubled over and Doug threw him violently onto the bed and wrestled one hand behind his back, then the other. The handcuffs clicked shut over his wrists and he growled a long string of obscenities.

"Search him," Alden said.

Doug ran his hands over Pedro's sides and waist, then pulled up his long shirt and removed a small stainless steel pistol from his waistband. He held it up.

"Here," Alden said, taking it from Doug and dropping it into his pocket. "Keep searching."

Doug ran his hands over Pedro's legs and reached into his pockets, producing a bag of what looked like marijuana, rolling papers, a lighter, and a thick wad of cash. He set them on the nightstand next to the bed.

"Get his belt," Alden said.

Doug have him a puzzled look, then undid the buckle of Pedro's brown leather belt and slid it out of his pant loops as the dealer thrashed beside the girl and swore. Alden tucked the pistol in his waistband and took the belt from Doug, then used it to bind the girl's wrists. She whimpered and Alden said, "I'm sorry."

"Who the fuck are you?" Pedro demanded.

Alden grabbed him and sat him upright on the bed.

"I said, who the fuck are you?"

Alden took a step back and looked at him.

"You deaf? I said—"

"I heard you," Alden interrupted.

Doug stepped away from the bed and moved beside Alden. His hands were shoved deep into his pockets and he glanced repeatedly at the door, sweat now glistening over his nose. Alden knew the expression on his face. He wanted to talk, but there was no time for that.

"You killed someone, Pedro," Alden said.

"I'll kill you. You're dead."

Alden's stomach tickled and turned over when he heard the words. Such desperate bravado. He was just talking, just making threats to distract himself. He knew now that he was prey. He knew that he'd been caught.

"You gave drugs to Tom," Alden said, "with the intention of killing a man that was bothering him."

"What?" Pedro said. "What the fuck are you talking about?"

"No need to play dumb with me."

"I ain't playin' dumb, asshole."

"Yes," Alden said, "you are, Pedro. You're trying to convince me that you had nothing to do with someone's death when I know that you did. Tom told me. That's why I'm here, Pedro."

"Yeah," the dealer scoffed, "and you think using my name is gonna break me down or something? Make me think you're my friend? Fuck you, bitch."

Alden smirked. "You're smarter than you look, I guess."

Pedro's eyes narrowed, but he seemed unable to think of a reply.

"Please," the girl said, "just let me go."

Alden looked at her. Tears had divided her cheeks with shiny lines. She was scared, shaking slightly and struggling against the leather belt that held her wrists together.

"You're going to tell me some things," Alden told her.

"What?"

"I'm going to ask you some questions, okay?"

She nodded.

"Is this stolen?" he asked, motioning to the DVD player.

"I didn't steal it."

"That's not what I asked."

She paused, then said, "Yeah, fine, it's stolen."

"Who stole it?"

She shook her head. A tear dropped from her cheek onto her jeans, leaving a small, dark circle.

Alden shivered, suddenly aware of the dull rush of cold air coming from the vent in the ceiling. His fingers felt clammy and bloodless. Some things, he thought, needed to be done. Sometimes you were forced into things. You could call it fate. You could call it whatever you wanted to call it, but sometimes bad things happened. Sometimes you had to do bad things to do good things—a sacrifice for a greater good. Sometimes you were the only one with the power to bring that good into being. It was about serving a higher purpose, and didn't he have the opportunity and the ability? The life of a thief for the honor of a friend.

Alden took the pistol from his waistband, stepped forward, brought the white dot in line with the girl's head from a few feet away, and pressed the trigger back twice.

He heard Doug's voice shout, "Shit!"

He heard Pedro's voice shout, "Fuck!"

He watched the girl's head jerk backward, but only slightly, as each round entered her skull. He watched her fall backward onto the mattress, collapsing heavily onto her bound hands. He saw her eyes roll upward. He saw the dark circle on her jeans. He observed the death as if from a distance. A subtle chill came over his chest, as if a cold wind had brushed skin that was mostly numb. He wondered if he would need more than three rounds to finish things.

There was a moment of stillness. Pedro had turned away and shut his eyes. Doug had stepped forward and dropped to one knee. Alden stared at the girl's body for a few seconds, then moved to the television and turned up the volume. Pedro's head turned to watch him. Alden stepped in front of the bed, grabbed the dealer by the collar, pressed the end of the suppressor to his head, and shoved him backward.

"No!" Pedro shouted.

Alden, now nearly on top of him, grabbed his short hair and shoved his face toward the girl's dead eyes. Her head had rolled to the side and her dull pupils were pointed at Pedro. He screamed and tried to squirm away, but

Alden held him down and forced him closer still, shoving the back of his head until his nose was touching the dead girl's.

"Look!" Alden commanded. "Look at her. You see that? You see what happens when people don't answer my questions? What happens when people lie to me? You want that to be you? You want to be like your friend?"

Pedro was crying. Tears were pooling on the side of his nose and he was gasping for air, his chest heaving under Alden's weight. He sobbed and tried to shake his head. Alden shoved his face once more into the corpse, then stood and took a step back from the bed.

Doug was sitting against the wall, watching with wide eyes as his hands shook. He grabbed his knees and swallowed, fighting his own tears. He didn't look at Alden.

"You're going to answer my questions," Alden said. "If you lie to me, you join your friend. Do you understand?"

Pedro's dark, tear-filled eyes narrowed and he glared at Alden. He was quiet for a time, staring, breathing hard, and sweating. There was blood on the comforter. He had cut his wrists struggling against the handcuffs. At length he said, "You're gonna kill me anyway."

Alden shrugged and said, "Tell me about Tips."

"Why?"

"I met with Tom," Alden said, "earlier today. He set up this meeting for me. He's still alive because he wasn't really the murderer. He was the tool, just an instrument used to deliver the drugs. He delivered *your* drugs, the Carfentanil, but I think this goes deeper. I think you were used, too."

Pedro took a deep breath.

"Am I right?" Alden asked. "Tell me about Tips. How was he involved in all of this?"

Pedro's gaze fell to the floor and he shook his head. "Tips didn't have nothin' to do with it."

"Tom said he went to Tips, then met you. You're not trying to lie to me, are you, Pedro?"

"Tips told me what to do, that's all."

"You're just saying that because you're afraid of what Tips would do to you if he found out what you told me."

Pedro's head both nodded and shook. "Shit, man, what do you expect?"

"It's not what I expect," Alden said, "but what I demand. I want honesty. I want the truth. Where did you get the Carfentanil?"

Pedro whispered, "Shit," then said, "I got it from Tips. He knows some vet or somethin'. I don't know."

Alden nodded. "Tom called Tips, Tips gave you the Carfentanil, and you gave the tainted heroin to Tom. Tom gave it to Mark. Is that right?"

"Yeah."

"Okay," Alden said. "Where's Tips?"

"What?"

"Where's Tips? Where does he live?"

"No way."

Alden brought the pistol on target and stepped forward. Pedro folded himself into a ball on the bed and screamed, "Burlington!"

Alden lowered the weapon. "Vermont?"

"Nah, man."

"Massachusetts?"

"Yeah," Pedro gasped, sitting again. "Yeah."

Alden looked back. Doug was standing again and leaning against the wall, his mouth open slightly and his eyes fixed on the girl's corpse. He was taking shallow breaths and his face was pale and slick with sweat. Alden wanted to say something to him, but suddenly Doug's eyes shifted and went wide. He pushed himself away from the wall, one arm outstretched. Alden felt the movement by the bed more than he saw it.

Pedro was moving fast. Alden twisted his head around and saw Pedro on his feet, half-crouched at the foot of the bed and leaning to the side. His feet shuffled, then took long steps toward the outside wall. Doug shouted something that Alden couldn't understand. The words, whatever they were, sounded muffled. His own racing heart dominated his senses. He watched Pedro lunging in slow motion. He watched the dealer's long shirt flapping as he threw himself into the air, a shoulder leading as he propelled himself sideways. He saw the grimace on Pedro's face as his body pushed the heavy curtains into the window and broke through. The sound of shattering glass was distant at first, but in an instant it was amplified as Alden's senses snapped into place.

He saw Doug running for the door, but didn't follow. He took two great strides toward the window and leapt through it himself, skidding on glass as his feet met the concrete. Pedro was there, half-prone and bleeding and struggling to stand. Alden reached down with his free hand and took hold of a bunch of Pedro's shirt. Doug had opened the door. Alden threw the dealer back through the window with a grunt, then took the key from his pocket and tossed it to Doug.

"Start the car!" he barked.

He saw Doug fumble the key as he vaulted back through the window. Pedro was on his back, rolling slightly from side to side. Alden stepped over him, stomped a foot onto his chest, brought the pistol on target, and fired two rounds into the dealer's head. The body jerked under his foot, then lay still. He took one step to the side and fired the last round. It punched a small hole beside Pedro's nose.

Casings, Alden thought. His eyes quickly scanned the floor. He heard the van's engine start outside. Where were they? He saw two next to Pedro's body, but where were the rest?

"Shit," he said.

He was out of time. He crossed the room, grabbed the roll of money on the nightstand, and left. He didn't shut the door behind him. Doug had backed the van out of the parking space. Alden ran to the passenger side and jumped inside.

"Go!" he shouted.

Doug hit the accelerator. The tires chirped on the asphalt and the minivan bounced over the rough parking lot toward the road. Alden twisted his head frantically around, looking through the windows, trying to see if there was anyone outside. He didn't think so, but he couldn't be sure. Doug turned onto the road.

"Speed limit," Alden said.

"What?" Doug asked loudly.

"Watch your speed."

"Yeah."

Alden looked at the pistol in his lap. He saw it in his own gloved hands. His hands were shaking. He coughed and blinked, then took the screwdriver, pliers, and file from one of the bags behind the seat. Breathing hard, he tore away the suppressor and disassembled the weapon. He removed the mainspring housing on the back of the grip, which released the slide from the frame. He used the pliers and one of the grip screws to remove the extractor, firing pin, and spring from the back of the slide. He set the small pieces in a cup holder and ran the rat-tail file through the barrel a few times.

"We're fucked," Doug said.

"Be quiet."

Alden took the extractor from the cup holder and ran it over the file, then did the same with the firing pin.

"What did you do?" Doug asked. "What the *fuck* did you do?"

Alden returned the pieces to the cup holder and replied, "It's what *we* did. We did what we said we were going to do."

"We're so fucked."

Alden folded his shaking hands and said slowly, "We are not fucked. We're going to get rid of the evidence. We're going to dispose of the gun and the file and everything else. We're going to ditch the clothes and the shoes and return the car with the rental plates. We're going to get rid of the stolen plates and we're going to go home and shave and take showers. Then we're going to meet at the bar, remember? We're going to be fine."

Doug's head was shaking. "Someone must've seen us."

"That's why we grew the beards and wore these clothes."

"What about the minivan?"

He was right about that, Alden thought. They left the wide road for a two-lane street that would take them back to the new route to the ferry. On the right side there was a camping area or some such place. Grassy fields and dirt tracks. Picnic tables and square, black grills. Alden pointed and said, "Pull in there."

"Why?"

"We're going to change the plates."

Doug pulled off the road onto the dirt path that led to a group of trees and parked. They got out of the minivan and Alden said, "Watch for anyone coming. Stand here. Block me."

The sun was still shining overhead, but the dappled shade was cool and breezy. Alden knelt and removed the rear license plate, then went around to the front of the vehicle and removed the front plate. He put them on the passenger seat and took the rental plates from beneath it, then attached them at the front and rear. He took the stolen New Hampshire plates from the seat and the suppressor from the floor and threw them into a nearby trash barrel.

"Get in the back," he said, "and change. I'll watch. Then I'll change and we can get rid of these clothes somewhere down the road."

Doug nodded dumbly and opened the side door on the minivan. He climbed inside and unzipped the coveralls.

Alden removed his gloves and motioned for Doug to do the same. He threw Doug's gloves away in the trash barrel, but kept his own in his pocket. He would need them one last time when they got rid of the—

A siren. Alden canted his head to one side and opened his mouth slightly. Yes, it was definitely a siren, but what kind? It sounded like an ambulance, but what if he was wrong? He looked into the back of the minivan and saw that Doug was out of his coveralls and had removed the clothes beneath.

"Underwear, too," Alden said. "Change it all. Hurry the hell up."

His heart was beating fast and his blood felt hot, as if the speed of the cells was creating uncomfortable friction in his veins. Would he be able to hear a siren at the hotel from here? No, probably not, but it could be a unit responding from a closer location. The siren was louder. It was getting closer.

When Doug had changed, Alden climbed into the back of the van. He sat next to the red toolbox and stripped naked. He put on his new underwear and the dark slacks and dress shirt from his other duffel. With sweat tickling his forehead, he took Pedro's gun and money from his used pants and put them in his pocket. Doug had left his old clothes on the floor and Alden put them, along with his own discarded garments, into one bag. He was about to climb out of the minivan when he remembered that he'd left his pair of latex gloves in the pocket of his other pants. He fished them out and stepped back onto the dirt parking area.

Standing at the rear of the van, he pulled the gloves on and opened the red toolbox. He dumped the bundles of cash into the other duffel bag, then closed the toolbox and set it down on the grass. He went back to the bag and looked inside for a moment, trying to estimate how much cash was there, then zipped the bag closed and said, "Let's go. I'll drive."

He and Doug climbed back into the minivan. Alden removed the handcuff key from the rental's ring and they left the recreation area for the road. Alden rolled down his window. He couldn't hear the siren anymore, but his blood was still racing hot and rough under his skin. He could feel sweat making his face slick and he saw that Doug's neck was lined with wet streaks.

"We'll be fine," Alden said.

The route to the ferry dock was mostly straight. When they reached the newly paved road and the speed limit increased, Alden checked his rear view mirror and saw that the nearest car was at least a quarter of a mile behind them. He reached into the cup holder and took the spring in hand, then tossed it through the open window. A moment later he did the same with the extractor, the firing pin, the key, and the tools. With the cup holder empty, he took off the gloves and stuffed them back into his pocket.

"What did you do?" Doug asked in a hoarse voice.

Alden glanced at him and saw that he was shaking his head and that his eyes were set behind a deep layer of tears.

"What did you do?" he asked again. "The girl. That girl."

"We didn't have a choice," Alden said. He felt a tightness in his throat and set his jaw, then added in a forceful tone, "No real choice."

"This was about Mark."

"I know that!" Alden shouted. "Do you think I forgot about him? Do you think I enjoyed what happened back there? Jesus, Doug!"

"What did she do?"

"What! I should've left her alive? I should've left her alive as a witness? What choice did I have? What choice did *we* have?"

"I didn't fuckin' kill her!"

"Just shut up!" Alden commanded. "Pull yourself together. We'll be at the dock soon. Get some composure."

Doug wiped his eyes on the sleeve of his t-shirt and took several long, shuddering breaths. He clenched and relaxed his hands and Alden saw them shaking each time the fingers fell out of a fist.

"Shit," Alden whispered.

"What?"

"Nothing. Just thinking."

The road curved and the speed limit dropped. Alden touched his foot to the brake pedal. Through the trees on the left he could see the dock and the lake beyond. The sky was mostly blue above them, but he could see denser clouds in the east. He turned the steering wheel and followed the curve toward one of the little white booths.

A middle-aged man with thick glasses was waiting at the window. Alden handed him the return ticket and received a boarding pass in return.

"Lane one," the man said.

Alden pulled into the first lane on the downhill slope. There were a few cars ahead of them. He looked at Doug, who was staring through the passenger side window at the wide lake, now a gentler blue under the exposed summer sky. The dock was empty, but the approaching ferry was already slowing and angling for the space. It bumped into place a few minutes later and the deckhands removed the ropes and let the cars onboard drive away. When it was clear, someone at the base of the hill waved for the line of waiting cards to approach.

Alden put the minivan in gear and followed the car in front of him down the curving hill to the flat space before the dock. He took his boarding pass in hand and stopped beside the collector. There was a stout, bearded man next to her with a clipboard. He stepped to the window as the girl took Alden's ticket.

"Are you familiar with our security procedures?" he asked.

Alden shook his head.

"I just need to check the back."

"It should be unlocked," Alden said.

The man moved to the back of the van.

"Fuck," Doug hissed. His hands were shaking violently and his face was pale and covered in sweat. He swallowed like he might be sick.

"Relax," Alden told him quietly. "There's nothing to find in the back. Relax."

In the rearview mirror, Alden saw the rear door swing open. The bearded man stood there for several seconds, his eyes moving over the duffel bags and the empty space. Then he closed the door and waved and said, "Thank you."

Alden waved and drove onto the ferry. The deckhand directed him to the far left lane, where he parked behind the other cars that had boarded ahead of him. He shifted into the parking gear and set the handbrake, then turned off the van.

"We're done," Doug said.

"We're okay," Alden replied. "When the ferry gets to the middle of the lake, we'll dump the frame and the slide. Then we dump the clothes on the way to my place, you return the van, we clean up, and we meet at the bar."

"How am I supposed to get home?"

Alden paused. How had he overlooked that?

"Well?" Doug insisted.

"I think you can afford a cab," Alden told him.

"And what about the money?"

"I don't know," Alden said. "I'll handle it. I'll find a place for it."

Doug was scratching his beard with both hands when the ferry lurched away from the dock and started its gradual turn toward the other side of the lake. Alden watched the sky over the cars in front of them. As the boat came around the clouds came into view, sliding gracefully from the right until their shadowed undersides dominated his vision.

"We're okay," Alden said again.

"That girl," Doug whispered. "She was—she couldn't have been— she was just a teenager."

Alden nodded. "I know."

"This isn't what I wanted."

"Yes," Alden said forcefully, "it is."

Doug looked back at him, his eyes narrow and his jaw tight.

"The guy who gave Mark the drugs is dead. The guy who supplied the drugs is dead. You wanted those things."

Doug opened his mouth to interrupt, but Alden raised a finger and continued, "No, you *did* want those things. You got those things. I told you from the beginning that this would be dangerous, so don't cry to me about how we're 'fucked' or 'done' or whatever. That girl is dead. Something happened that you didn't want to happen, but that doesn't change the things that you wanted. It doesn't mean you never wanted them. You wanted them and you got them. That's it. Shit happens. We have to deal with that."

"Oh," Doug said, straightening in his seat, "it's that easy for you, huh? You fuckin' kill a teenage girl and it's that easy. Shit just happens! Well, *you* killed that girl. *We* didn't do anything. You decided that she had to die. You didn't get that idea from me!"

Alden shook his head and said, "Calm down. We have work to do. We're okay and we're going to be okay, but we're not safe yet."

Doug's face had gone red and his hands were trembling. Alden took a deep breath and shook his head again.

"What?" Doug snapped.

"If you don't keep it together," Alden said, "I can't relax. I need to relax. I need to think and keep things on track. The girl was a bad thing. I know that, okay? Jesus, how could I not know that? I made the decision. You're right about that, but it wasn't a decision I wanted to make. I had to make it. If we let—if I let her go, what do you think she would've done? We *would* be fucked."

Doug's chest was heaving, but he nodded. "What now?"

Alden took the gloves from his pocket and put them on, then reached over the console and under Doug's seat to retrieve the pistol's slide and frame. He held them close to his body and said, "We need to get rid of these. I'll throw them over. Just block for me and tell me when I'm clear to toss them, okay? Walk in front of me to the back of the boat."

"Okay."

They got out of the minivan. Alden kept his hands low and Doug came around the back to lead the way. They walked beside the two cars that had parked behind them, then across the open deck to the stern of the ferry. The wind blew against the back of Alden's neck and made his shirt flutter against his skin. It cooled his sweat and made him shiver.

"Go to the right," Alden said, "where the wall ends."

The side of the boat ended near three stout ropes stretched across the open stern of the boat. Alden stopped near the end of the waist-high wall and leaned against it.

"Move around the other side of me," he said. "Block the view."

Doug stepped around him and mimicked his casual pose.

"Anyone looking?" Alden asked.

"No," Doug replied, "I don't think so. You should be good."

Alden lifted the frame and slide to the level of the wall, craned his neck to examine the view past Doug, and dropped the pieces of the pistol overboard. They splashed into the undulating lake, but Alden didn't watch them go. Instead, he turned back toward the bow, removed the gloves, and walked to the minivan. Doug followed behind, still breathing fast but now fighting a smile.

"What?" Alden asked as they entered the van.

"That's it, right? All the evidence is gone."

"No," Alden said. "We still have the clothes, remember?"

"Right, right. Where do we ditch them?"

Alden examined Doug's face, flushed but showing an easy smile. The suddenness of the mood swing made his stomach twist uncomfortably and he shifted in his seat.

"We can take secondary roads back to my place," he replied. "We'll find a quiet place on the way and toss them in the trash."

"Good," Doug said, nodding and almost bouncing as he turned forward in his seat. "Good."

Alden drove past the onramp to the Interstate and stopped at a red light. When it turned green he took a right and drove on. The landscape was still dominated by fields and glades here, but that changed quickly. A gas station at the bottom of a long, steep hill introduced them to areas dotted with flat parking lots around clusters of commercial development—asphalt and corrugated steel marked with large signs occasionally punctuated with neon.

Alden turned left at an intersection. They passed a small strip mall and he considered stopping, but decided against it. The roadside became lined with trees that sheltered houses at regular intervals. Traffic was heavier here, flowing quickly on the two-lane road. It curved and rose and dipped. Alden checked his speed. Just over the limit. He picked his foot up for a moment to slow down.

Several minutes later he came to an intersection with a wider, busier road. He stopped at a yield sign and waited for a long line of cars to pass by before he could continue. There was a sign for a hotel ahead. He drove past it, then turned left across the traffic for a side street. It connected to the parking lot of the large, multistory building. It was painted light green with brick accents. The lot was mostly empty.

Alden slowed the minivan and drove around the hotel. There were two large, green dumpsters at the back, beside a metal door that showed rust at the hinges. He stopped the van in front of them.

"Okay," he said to himself.

"Okay," Doug replied.

Alden looked at him, then got out of the minivan. He took the latex gloves from his pocket and opened the back. He looked at the two duffel bags for a few seconds, then took the one containing the clothes and unzipped it. He shoved the gloves inside, zipped it closed, and carried it to the nearest dumpster. He lifted the black plastic lid with one hand and tossed the bag inside with the other. He heard trash bags crinkle beneath it before he let the lid drop.

"Okay," he said again when he was back in the van. "Almost done."

"Almost?"

"One more thing before we drop this thing off."

Alden drove around the side of the two-story, brick bookstore and looked over the parking lot. No spaces. He continued through the lot and looked at the concrete parking ramp on his right. Too exposed. He passed it and turned into another lot beside it, then spotted the downward ramp into the single-level parking garage beneath.

Even in the light of the cloudy afternoon the garage was dark, lit only with dim orange bulbs behind stained plastic. Alden parked the van beneath a burned out light and turned off the engine.

"What's this about?" Doug asked.

"We're going to wipe it down," Alden said. "Then you drive. You'll need to pay attention to what you and I touch, but you shouldn't have much to wipe down when you drop it off. Just the wheel and the handles and whatever. Wipe it down before you drop off the key."

Doug nodded. "No problem."

"Drop me here," Alden said.

Doug pulled over to the side of the road. They were a couple of streets away from Alden's townhouse. The sky was mostly clear and the sun was bright against the champagne paint of the minivan. Alden got out. He wiped the inside door handle with his sleeve, then went to the back. He took the bag of money from inside and shut the hatch, then wiped the latch. He slung the bag over his shoulder and took Pedro's wad of money from his pocket.

"Here," he said at the driver's side window.

Doug took the cash and said, "Keep the rest of that safe."

"I'll figure something out. You okay doing the rest of this?"

"Yeah," Doug said, shifting in his seat. "Drop off the van. Wipe it down. Cab it home. Shave and shower. Meet you at the bar at ten."

Alden nodded. "See you."

"Yeah."

Alden watched him drive away, then walked toward his house with the black duffel bag over his shoulder. There was money inside, Alden thought. Drug money. Dirty money. Some of it might have been the money Mark had used to buy the drugs that had killed him.

He walked faster, trying to outpace the painful, irregular rhythm of his heart. Some of it was probably Mark's money. Alden shook his head, willing the thought away. He needed to decide what he was going to do with it. It would probably fit in one of the large safe deposit boxes, he thought, but didn't you have to register for those? Of course you did. You probably needed identification or an account at the bank or something. No, he couldn't bring it to a bank even for the safe deposit box. He would have to think of something else.

He reached the door to his townhouse and felt his pocket, then swore. All that planning and he'd forgotten his house key inside. He hefted the bag on his shoulder and walked to his car in the covered space across from his walkway. He set the bag down and knelt beside the car, feeling under the back door on the driver's side for the little plastic box that was magnetically attached to the frame. He opened it and a key dropped into his palm. He took it and the bag to the townhouse and went inside.

He shut the door behind him, locked the deadbolt, and took off his shoes. He let the duffel bag fall to the floor with a thump and walked into the kitchen. He turned on the faucet and cupped his hands under the water, then drank. His hands smelled like latex.

He turned off the faucet and leaned against the edge of the counter. The sun was shining through a gap in the clouds and he squinted as a car drove by and reflected searing light at his eyes. He blinked and went to his office.

The computer was on. He turned on the monitor and moved the mouse to get rid of the screensaver. The web browser was open and waiting for him to click a purple button that read, "Submit."

He clicked and waited. The next screen confirmed that the job application had been sent and he closed the browser. He took a deep breath and went back to the kitchen. He opened the refrigerator, then closed it before looking inside. He wasn't very hungry.

The air felt thick and smelled like dust. He went to the living room and turned on the air conditioner, but didn't wait to feel the cool air. He went to the bathroom upstairs instead. The weight of Pedro's gun seemed suddenly heavier and he took it from his pocket and set it on top of the hamper. Then he undressed, letting the clothes fall into a pile on the floor. He set his socks on either side of the pile so he wouldn't have to sort one from the other when he put them back on.

He used the toilet and turned on the shower. His hand came to rest on the toilet's handle, but he removed it before flushing. It would make the water in the shower too hot and he'd have to wait. He could flush after he washed up.

He looked in the mirror. It was already beginning to show condensation at the edges. He ran a hand over his beard. He took his electric razor from beneath the sink and used the trimmer. Short pieces of hair fell into the white basin and gathered around the edge. He closed the trimmer and used the regular blades to remove the stubble that remained. He had to empty the razor three times. He tapped the shavings into the sink.

He examined his reflection. His cheeks looked smooth, but the skin on his throat was red and there was a small spot of blood just under his chin. He wiped the tiny drop away with his thumb and licked it off. It tasted bitter and metallic. It reminded him of an old skeleton key his parents had kept on top of a dresser in their bedroom. He used to take it and put it in his mouth until the taste became too much. Then he would put the key back and rub his tongue against the roof of his mouth until the bitterness had faded.

He closed his eyes and saw straight blonde hair. He saw blue eyes, blue like the water of the lake under the clear sky—a dark, deep blue. He saw them go shallow. He heard her voice.

"Jen," she'd said. Jennifer. Who had she been? Who had she left behind? Alden's legs trembled and he sat, naked, on the bathroom floor. The hiss of the shower filled his ears. He opened his eyes and looked at the steam gathering above him. The three round light bulbs over the mirror were glowing through the haze. He let himself down onto his side and stared at the wall.

"Jennifer," he whispered.

A tear pooled in the corner of his eye at the bridge of his nose. He blinked and it dropped onto the white linoleum. He closed his eyes and sobbed once, then took a deep, shuddering breath and rose. He wiped his eyes and looked at the mirror, but there was no reflection to be seen through the fog.

VI

Alden saw Doug's SUV in the bar's lot and parked next to it. He got out and stretched his back. There were a few people on the deck on the building's left side, already drunk and boisterous. Alden walked under the lighted green awning and went inside. He checked his watch. It was just after ten o'clock.

A plucky folk tune was playing on the jukebox and Alden frowned. He took the two steps up to the gritty floor in front of the bar and saw Doug sitting halfway down. Alden's frown turned to a scowl. Doug's girlfriend was sitting next to him, flipping her auburn hair and smiling.

Alden slid onto the seat next to Doug and said, "Hey Tiffany."

"Hey Aldy."

Doug looked his way, almost startled, and asked, "How's it going?"

"It's going."

"Find a new job yet?" Tiffany asked.

"Not yet, but I sent my resume out a few times today, so we'll see how that goes. What about you?"

"I just started at another bank," she said. "Just part-time until I'm done with school next year."

The bartender approached and Doug said, "He'll have a glass of rum."

"No, actually," Alden said with a wry smile. "Jameson neat, please."

Doug gave a long, low whistle and his fingers tapped rapidly on the bar. "Changing it up, huh?"

Alden shrugged and said, "Just not in the mood for something that sweet, I guess. What's got you all worked up?"

Doug's eyes widened slightly and he opened his mouth to speak, but stayed silent and Tiffany said, "He's been antsy all night."

Alden saw that Doug's beer was almost empty. "Have another one," he suggested. "I'm sure Tiffany can drive you home."

"Sure," she said. "I'm not having any more. They'd just go right through me, anyway."

She got up and walked toward the bathrooms. Alden watched her go, then turned to Doug and asked, "You okay?"

The bartender put the glass of whiskey on the bar and Alden slid it close, but didn't drink. He looked at Doug looking at him, eyes tinted red and hands still tapping.

"Can you hold it together?" Alden asked quietly.

Doug paused, then nodded. "Yeah. I'm okay."

"You sure?"

"I'll be okay."

"Why's Tiffany here?"

"You asked her to come a few weeks ago," Doug said, "and she couldn't then. She thought the offer was still good."

"Had to be tonight."

"I know. I don't even want to see her right now."

Alden took a sip of the whiskey and said, "Just put up with it. I'm only going to have this, then leave. Keep her happy. Just don't let her think anything's wrong."

"I should tell her I don't feel good."

"No. That's something wrong. Just put up with it."

Tiffany returned to the bar and Alden gave Doug a sharp look, then smiled and drank most of the liquor in his glass.

"Getting a fast start?" Tiffany asked.

"More like a quick finish," Alden replied. "I have to drop off a few applications tomorrow morning, so it can't be a very late night. I just wanted to stop by to say hello."

"That's too bad."

Alden shrugged and tilted his head side to side. "Well, don't feel down on my account. Feel free to get this guy as drunk as you want. Maybe play a few games of pool."

She laughed and he gave her a wink.

"Oh, sure," Doug said. "You're just trying to get me hung over."

"You work the nightshift. If you're not over it by then, you're a bigger wuss than I thought! Can't even hold a few beers." Alden exaggerated a shake of his head. "Pretty sad."

"I'll have another one," Doug said to the bartender, waving his mostly empty bottle. Then he looked at Alden and said, "I'd like to see you go one for one with me, pal."

"Anytime."

"Sure. What do you weigh? Ninety pounds?"

"Hey," Alden said, "I've got a little thing called tolerance on my side. Don't underestimate me." He threw back the rest of the whiskey and set the glass down hard to punctuate his claim.

"Someone could *only* underestimate you," Doug said with a sneer.

Alden grinned and Tiffany held back a laugh.

"What?" Doug asked.

"Unless you were trying to seduce me," Alden said, "I think you meant someone could only *over*estimate me."

Doug finished his beer and said, "Oh, fuck you both."

Alden leaned back to look past Doug at Tiffany, then said with a half-smile, "I'm up for it if you are."

Tiffany laughed as Alden stood and put ten dollar bill on the bar.

"You're a bastard," Doug said with snort.

"Yeah, probably," Alden replied. "I'll see you guys later. Let me know if you have a good day off this week. Maybe we'll grab a couple of drinks downtown for once."

Doug nodded. "Okay."

"See you, Aldy," Tiffany said.

Alden waved as he took a few steps backward. He gave them another wink and turned, trotted down the steps, and pushed through the door into the humid air outside. He walked to his car and started it, but didn't put it in gear.

Doug was nervous. That was normal, right? It should be expected after what they'd done. Alden let his head fall back against the headrest. If that was normal, why didn't he feel nervous? Shouldn't he be worried about the police? The evidence they'd left behind? The casings in the hotel?

Alden shook his head. No, there was no reason to be nervous about the casings. Even if they found the gun at the bottom of the lake, there was no way to link it to those casings. Doug wasn't worried about that, anyway, was he? No, Doug was worried about something much less concrete. Alden closed his eyes and listened to the old 90's Prozac rock on the radio.

His mind drifted back to the private school that had dominated his teenage years with Doug and Mark. That place was the source of Doug's fear. Alden was sure of it. Doug wasn't worried about arrest, or if he was, that concern was dwarfed by his fear of God. He didn't practice regularly anymore, but he still went to church once in a while and on Christmas and Easter. He still believed and so did Tiffany.

That was how it worked, Alden thought. So many years with all that religion so close led you to one of two ends; some kids believed for the rest of their lives and some kids stopped believing. Alden sighed. How could he calm Doug's fears? He could find some relevant passages in the Bible, but that was pointless. For every quote that supported their acts of vengeance, Doug could find one that condemned them. Alden leaned forward and looked up through the windshield at the stars visible between the clouds.

"You really mixed things up with that New Testament business," he said dryly, then sat back. "Wish you still talked to us lowly men, too."

He sat in silence for a moment, wishing for but not expecting a great, booming voice to offer guidance. He breathed a laugh and put the car into gear. Maybe God was out there, watching and judging, but what did it matter?

Alden pulled out of the parking lot and glanced again at the stars, then whispered, "You want to watch and judge, that's your business. Just stay out of mine."

Alden woke up eight minutes before his clock was set to go off. He reached over and turned off the alarm, then sat up and took a deep breath. He went to his closet and took out a pair of khakis and a white shirt, then took some underwear from the bureau and walked to the bathroom.

He showered quickly and dressed, then went downstairs. He'd left the air conditioner running overnight and it was pleasantly cool when he made himself a bowl of cereal in the kitchen. He brought it into the living room and turned on the television to watch the forecast while he ate. It was supposed to be hot, but not unseasonably so. A few clouds now and then, but a nice day overall. Alden drank the milk from his bowl, then rinsed it in the kitchen and set it on the dish rack.

He went to his office and turned on the computer. When the operating system had loaded, he launched his web browser and went to the homepage for the local newspaper. He scanned the headlines, but saw nothing about Tom or any other crimes. In a city so small, that would be big news. Definitely front page.

He had to use a search engine to find the local paper for Plattsburgh. The front page was cleanly built of white and blue, with the top story listed on the left side of the page. It read, "Two Shot Dead in Plattsburgh Hotel." Beside it was a link to a story about a fundraiser.

Alden clicked on the title of the top story and read the article. Police were asking anyone with information to call them. That was to be expected. There was no mention of the victims' identities. Alden frowned. He was hoping to find out more about the girl. The article mentioned that large quantities of several drugs had been found in the hotel room and the car outside. There was nothing about witnesses and no description of the minivan or of suspects. That was probably good, but the police might have kept it away from the press.

Alden closed the browser and went back to the living room. He looked at the stairs and thought about getting his pistol from the bedroom, but he wasn't dressed to conceal it and he decided not to bother. He took his wallet and keys from the kitchen counter and moved for the front door, but stopped when he bent down for his shoes. The black duffel bag was still there.

He stared at the bag as he put on his shoes, then picked it up and carried it outside. He couldn't keep it at home. He put it in the trunk of his car, then slid behind the wheel and drove out of his neighborhood.

It was a ten minute drive to the fitness center he used. He parked, popped the trunk, and stepped outside. The morning air was still cool and the light was still tinged with orange. He lifted the trunk lid and unzipped the duffel bag. The money lay in a jumble. He took several hundred dollars in various denominations and put it in his pocket, then zipped the bag closed and took it out. He shut the trunk and walked into the large, tan-colored building.

He went to the front desk, behind which sat a happy blonde girl staring at a desk calendar. She looked up at him and said, "Hi. Can I help you?"

"Yeah," Alden said. "I forgot my lock. Do you have any here?"

"Oh, yeah. We have them in the shop."

"On the left?" Alden asked, pointing to the door that led farther into the gym.

"Yep."

"Thanks."

He walked to the door and held the fitness center pass on his keys to sensor beside the door. The sensor beeped and he opened the door and walked into the hallway. The door to the shop was just a short way down. He walked inside and smiled to the employee behind the counter. He was a young guy, just a kid in his teens.

"Morning," Alden said. "I need a lock, please."

"Sure," the clerk said. He took down a combination lock with a blue face from a peg hook behind the counter and scanned it at the register. "It's eight dollars and fifty-eight cents."

"Wow," Alden said, fishing through his pocket. "You guys make a killing on those."

The kid smiled awkwardly and Alden handed him a ten dollar bill. He took his change and left. The locker room was down the hall. He went to the corner of the room and looked at the locker numbers. He walked through the rows for several seconds, then stopped when he saw locker number 148.

"Forty-eight," he mouthed.

He wouldn't forget that number for the rest of his life. He opened the locker and put the duffel bag inside, then tore open the lock's package. He looked at the small piece of paper with the combination on it and whispered the numbers a few times. He tried the combination and opened the lock, then used it to secure the locker.

On his way out of the room he took his cell phone from its holder and held it up to his ear. As he walked out of the hallway and into the lobby, he said in an urgent voice, "I'm just leaving now. I'll be there as soon as I can." He gave an apologetic look to the girl behind the desk and went outside. He kept the phone to his ear until he was in his car. He started the engine and drove out of the lot. It was fifteen minutes to the nearest office supply store and he still needed a digital shredder.

At home, after the software was installed on his computer, Alden transferred his resume, a few folders of digital photographs, and a couple of old college papers onto a flash drive. He looked through the rest of the folders on his hard drive, but found nothing of value and began the process of formatting with his new software. He'd read somewhere that data could still be recovered from the drive even after it had been swept clean once or twice, so highly sensitive data was usually overwritten a few times. Didn't the Pentagon require three or four passes? He couldn't remember, but assuming it was four, he set the program to make eight passes.

The format would take a long time. He left the office and sat on his couch. Across the room, tucked between two large textbooks on his bookcase, was the "technical manual" they'd used as a reference. He stared at it for several seconds, then went to the shelf and took it down. He'd already disposed of the legal cases and the other documents he'd printed, but he'd overlooked the book. It was evidence, or could be, however circumstantial. He would have to throw it away when he went out.

He set the book on the coffee table and went to the kitchen. His stomach grumbled and he had a hand on the door of the refrigerator when his cell phone rang in the other room. He went back to the coffee table and picked it up. It was Doug. He answered, "Hey, what's up?"

Doug's voice sounded raspy and thin and he slurred a little. "Not much."

"Doesn't sound that way."

"Yeah, well, listen," Doug said. "You got time to talk?"

Alden felt a tingle of annoyance wind over the back of his shoulders and he sat on the couch. "About yesterday?"

"Yeah."

"What about it?"

"What?" Doug asked, his voice high with disbelief. "What do you mean? All of it. Fuck! We killed three people."

"You wanted to kill two of them, remember?"

There was a pause on the other end of the line, then Doug said, "I didn't know it would be like that. Like this. And the girl. Shit, the girl."

Alden leaned forward and put his head in one hand. "I know. Believe me, I know. That hit me hard, too."

"What, it's not *hitting* you hard? You're over it now?"

Alden thought about that for a few seconds. Was he over it? Last night he'd collapsed at the thought of her. Today he'd hardly thought about her at all until now. Was he over it, or was his mind just keeping him safe with some artificial distance?

"I don't know," Alden said. "I don't know what to think yet."

"It's killing me, you know? I already called out of work. There's no way I can go in there like this."

Alden sat straight. "You have to go in. You can't break routine like that. Not yet, okay? You just have to do it."

"I can't, man," Doug said, his voice cracking. "I didn't sleep at all last night. I couldn't wait for Tiffany to leave. My hands won't stop shaking and I can't stop thinking about all of it. Sometimes my whole body shakes. I just can't do it. I just can't."

"Relax. Just take a minute and relax." Alden stood and paced. "We were both there when they died, that's true, but who pulled the trigger? Who really killed them? You killed Tom, but he deserved it more than anyone, right? Pedro and Jennifer are my weight to carry, not yours."

He heard Doug groan and start to cry. Shit, Alden thought. He shouldn't have used her name. He took a deep breath and tried to keep himself calm. He needed to be calm if he was going to keep Doug calm.

"That was her name?" Doug asked. "How do you know that?"

"She told us," Alden said, "but it doesn't matter. Like I said, that's my problem, not yours, and I'll deal with it. You killed someone, but he deserved it. He deserved worse than what he got. He murdered Mark."

"I know, but Jesus, I mean—"

"Doug, stop. What's the point of all this worrying? What's it going to accomplish?"

"You think I'm trying to accomplish something? I don't want to feel like this! I felt like I couldn't breathe when I was in the shower this morning! I just want it to go away. Just go away, you know?"

"I know."

"So what do I do?"

Alden shook his head and stared at the air conditioner. "I don't know, man. You still have your meds from your back thing?"

"Some."

"What were they? Vicodin?"

"Yeah, I think so."

"Take one and go to bed. Get some sleep."

Doug sighed and said quietly, "Okay."

"I'll talk to you later."

"Yeah."

Alden closed his phone and set it back on the coffee table. He rubbed his temples and moved in front of the air conditioner, letting the air make his skin uncomfortably cool while he looked at the long grass of his lawn. He stood there until the cold became unbearable, then wandered to the kitchen. He looked through the cupboards, but he didn't feel like soup.

He went back to the coffee table for his cell phone, then took his wallet and keys and went to his car. He didn't know where he was going. Maybe he would eat out or maybe he would go to the grocery store. Probably the store. It would be cheaper and he'd have more than cereal or soup at the house.

He started his car and considered stopping by the cemetery while he was out, but decided against it. The gravesite was too close to Tom's house and there hadn't been anything in the paper this morning. He didn't want to be near the scene when it was found.

The phone didn't ring again until Alden was watching Leno. He took the cool brown bottle of beer from between his legs and set it on the coffee table, picked up the phone, and turned off the television. The room went dark without the glow of the screen. Alden looked at Doug's name on the front of his phone for a few seconds before he answered.

"Hey."

"Hey," Doug said on the other end, his voice nearly drowned out by a wash of what sounded like wind.

"Where are you?" Alden asked.

"Outside. Tiffany's sleeping. I didn't want to wake her up."

"How're you doing?"

"Okay," Doug said.

Alden could hear tightness in his friend's voice and thought he was probably crying. "You sure?"

Doug swore, but it was inaudible over the wind.

"Hey," Alden said, "come on. Talk to me. What's going on?"

"I can't handle this. I can't."

"Did you get any sleep?"

"Some, yeah."

"Then talk to me. What's going on?"

"The girl."

Alden sat back and looked up into the darkness. "I know."

"You said her name was Jennifer," Doug said, breathing shakily over the wind. "I had a dream about her."

Alden didn't know what to say and waited for Doug to continue.

"I shot her. I shot her and shot her, but she just kept crying and looking at me like, 'Why are you doing this?' And I just kept shooting her and she got so bloody, but she just kept looking at me that way."

"You didn't kill her. I did."

"Going there was our decision!"

"Yeah," Alden said, "that's true. We decided to go after Pedro, but we didn't know she would be there. There was no plan in place for that. I had to make a decision. I improvised and I killed her, you didn't."

"It doesn't matter," Doug said, starting to sob.

Alden looked at the thin line of light on the carpet. Why wasn't he broken up about it like Doug? They had made the decision to go to the hotel, but it was true that Doug had nothing to do with the girl's death—Jennifer's death. He knew her name. He shot her twice in the head and what? A few tears on the bathroom floor. Was that his penance for such a sin?

"Shit," Doug said, sniffing.

"What?"

"The lights are on in the kitchen. Tiffany must be up. She's probably looking for me. I have to go."

"It's not your fault," Alden said, but he wasn't sure Doug had heard him. The sound of the wind had gone by the time he'd finished speaking.

He put the phone on the coffee table, turned on the television, and took a long drink of beer. He watched the talk show and drank. Maybe his brain was shutting out his response to killing the girl. Maybe he would have a break down sooner or later, or an ulcer or a heart attack, but he couldn't feel anything coming. Until he could, it was no matter.

Alden went to his computer again the next morning and spent a few hours installing his operating system and the programs he used most. He transferred his media files and old papers back onto the hard drive, and with a cup of instant coffee beside the monitor, pulled up the website for the local newspaper.

The top story was titled, "Murder in the North End." There was a picture of the house with an ambulance and a police cruiser nearby. Alden read the article carefully. The victim's body had been discovered by his girlfriend, who was working with the police. Good, Alden thought. It served that bitch right to walk in on that scene. Reading on, Alden saw that the police were declining to comment about the details of the killing or any suspects under investigation, but were emphasizing the brutal nature of the crime. Drugs had been found in the house, but there was no detailed information. As with the article in Plattsburgh's local paper, police were seeking information from anyone willing to give it.

Alden read the article several times. When he was satisfied he'd recall the few details, he navigated to the site he used regularly for his online job search. He took a sip of coffee and checked his watch. He'd give it an hour, then go to the gym to check on the money and spend some time exercising. He felt like being active.

He ran hard, his legs falling in a steady rhythm that happened to match the beat of the hard rock coming through his ear buds. The digital display on the front of the machine showed six miles in just over forty-five minutes. His cell phone was resting in the tray beside the numbers. He couldn't hear it ring over the music, but saw the front screen light up with Doug's name. He put his feet on the sides of the treadmill and stopped it.

He wiped his forehead on the sleeve of his shirt, removed the ear buds from his ears, and answered the phone.

"Hey," he said breathlessly, "I was just running. What's up?"

"Alden, man," Doug said, "something's wrong."

"What do you mean?"

"You know they found the body?"

"I saw that."

"I think their friends are looking for us."

Alden closed his eyes and asked, "What are you talking about?"

"This car's been driving by," Doug said. "It's been by, fuck, I don't know how many times."

"What kind of car?"

"Like a Civic or an Accent or something."

Alden looked down and a drop of sweat fell from his hair onto the treadmill. It was probably nothing. There was no way to connect them with the crimes unless a witness had come forward, right?

"Where are the plates from?" Alden asked.

"What?"

"What state are the license plates from?"

"I don't know. They're white, I think."

Alden sighed. "Okay, look. It's probably just someone who got lost. Maybe they're just looking for the right road or the right house. It's probably nothing, okay? Relax."

"Someone's going to come looking."

"They might," Alden said. "They probably will, but there's nothing for them to find. We're safe, okay? We made sure of that. You know that."

"I don't know, man. I just keep seeing this goddamn car."

"Okay," Alden said, "okay. Your Kimber is fixed, right?"

"Yeah."

"You have it in condition one?"

"What?"

"Cocked and locked?" Alden said.

"Yeah, I think so."

"Make sure, then keep it close, but just in case. This car is nothing, okay? Just keep it close if it makes you feel better."

"Fuck!" Doug yelled. "I'm not fucking kidding, okay? Something is seriously wrong here!"

"What do you want me to do? Do you want me to come out there and see for myself? Do you think that'll help? You're just being paranoid, okay? The car is nothing."

"Shit," Doug in a calmer voice. "Shit, man, I don't know. I just don't feel right. Something's not right."

"What do you want me to do?"

"I don't know. I'm just scared, I guess. I almost called the cops."

Alden's breath stopped for a moment, then he said in a harsh, hushed tone, "That's not an option. That is *not* an option. Understand?"

"I know. I didn't. I just, I mean, I thought about it."

Alden shook his head. "It's not an option."

"I know, really. I'm just nervous."

"Do you want me to come out there?"

There was a pause, then Doug said, "No."

"But you still think something's wrong," Alden said flatly.

"Something feels wrong. I don't know."

"The car is nothing," Alden said again. "We're safe. We really are safe, okay? Relax. Did you sleep last night?"

"Some."

Alden got off the treadmill and took his MP3 player as he walked toward the locker rooms.

"Still there?" Doug asked.

"Yeah," Alden said, "I'm just leaving the gym. How much sleep did you get?"

"An hour or two."

"And that means what, really? An hour?"

A pause, then, "Maybe."

"Take another Vicodin," Alden said, "and get some sleep. Call me if anything really happens, okay?"

Doug said, "Okay," but his voice was weak.

"Are you going to work tonight?"

"Yeah," Doug grumbled. "I'll be there."

"What time will you get home?"

"Probably around eight o'clock."

"And when does Tiffany usually leave for work?"

"Around eight-thirty."

"Okay," Alden said, "I'll stop by a little after that. Maybe nine o'clock or so, okay? We can talk about it."

"Yeah, that sounds good. I really need to talk."

"I'll be there."

"Thanks."

"No problem. See you then."

Alden closed his phone and pushed open the door to the locker room. Doug was worried about nothing, but he was still worried, and that was a problem. How close had he come to calling the police? What would he have told them? Alden shook his head and undressed. This whole ordeal was probably more dangerous now than it had been when they were going after Tom and Pedro.

He had to see to Doug's mental state, but what could he do? He had to admit to himself that he didn't know much about how to handle the present problem. If Doug had called the police, they both could've ended up in prison. He had to see how far down Doug had fallen, but he also had to take care of himself, just in case. He had to prepare for the worst.

Chris Tucker was on Leno to promote an upcoming movie with Jackie Chan. Alden had seen the first and second films, but he was skeptical of a third movie in the series. He would probably see it anyway. Jackie Chan was always good for a few interesting action sequences, no matter how bad the rest of the movie might be.

To his surprise, Doug didn't call. He was left in peace to sip a bottle of beer and relax. Sometimes, Alden thought, it felt good to be unemployed and unmotivated. During a commercial break he drank what remained of his beer and went to the kitchen for another. He could hear a melodramatic advertisement playing in the living room. He returned in time to see a young girl looking distressed on the screen, weeping that marijuana had ruined the life of a friend.

Alden gave the screen a twisted half-smile. People never looked far enough. They saw a problem and only investigated until they found a cause, but that was rarely the root of it. The drugs didn't magically appear in the hands of those willing to sell it for profit. They were manufactured illegally or diverted from legal manufacturers. The people who did those things at the highest levels—or perhaps the lowest, Alden thought—were organized and methodical. They were careful businessmen interested in running a profitable business.

Tom had been an insignificant part of the overall structure. Pedro, too, had been insignificant. Both of their places would be quickly filled by others seeking a quick buck. Maybe there were people already prepared to take over their roles. So, Alden wondered, what about those people?

They didn't matter. Tom and Pedro had been directly involved in murdering Mark. Whoever took their places probably didn't know anything about what had happened. Maybe they wondered why the jobs had opened in such a way, but they probably didn't care; a software engineer probably didn't care why the guy before him had been fired.

Despite the obvious distance between the dealers' replacements and Mark's death, Alden felt a subtle compellation to seek them out. He wanted to know who they were and what they did when they weren't exchanging dope for cash. He wanted to know what they looked like and with whom they were connected. How did they make their deals? How much cash did they carry on them? How much did they keep at home?

Alden took a deep breath and settled back into the couch cushions. The replacements had nothing to do with Mark, but they had everything to do with the other people addicted to the products. There were people who followed in Mark's footsteps every day. Maybe their deaths weren't intentional, but they were certainly accepted as a matter of business for those who dealt them the chemicals that would deliver them to Death's door. And they had families and friends, right? Weren't those people entitled to justice? Didn't the replacement dealers and suppliers deserve the fate that had been forced on Tom and Pedro?

Alden sighed. Yes, they deserved the same fate, but it wasn't his business to deliver it. His obligation had been to Mark, and even that had caused unintended damage. Jennifer shouldn't have had to die. She had been in the wrong place at the wrong time, Alden thought, and that was all.

He thought about her. The shocked expression on her face was quick to appear before his mind's eye. The way her eyes stared after the bullets had bounced around inside her skull, tearing apart her brain, was easy to recall. He'd lost control after that. He'd used the opportunity to frighten Pedro, but nothing had gone as he'd intended. Everything had been improvised and it could've easily resulted in their apprehension.

"Doesn't matter," Alden told himself.

He turned his attention back to the television and decided he'd have one more beer, then go to bed. He wanted to make it to Doug's place early.

The next morning, Alden settled into his office chair and went through the bottom drawer of his desk. It was unorganized—just a heap of miscellaneous things he'd never bothered to sort. Two old textbooks were pushed against the side of the drawer, both from his first year of college. One covered basic criminal law and the other simple concepts of social deviance. The class requiring the latter had been mindlessly easy, but the teacher had been good. Former FBI, he thought.

Atop a shoebox were three small notepads, their covers bent and scratched from once-constant use. Alden picked up the green one. It was the first notepad he'd used as a deputy. He opened it and flipped through several pages, stopping at a brief note. It was a messily scribbled name and address with a phone number written vertically on the right side. Below was written, "Fake identification for James Hodgetts." Alden tore the page from the notepad and put it in his pocket.

Doug met him at the door. He was dressed in a gray t-shirt and frayed blue jeans. His eyes were full atop dark half-circles. He looked at Alden through the screen and shook his head.

"You didn't need to come out here."

"I wanted to come out here," Alden said.

"Why?" Doug asked, holding the screen door open.

Alden stepped inside and said, "We're in this together."

The front door led them immediately to the kitchen and Doug sat down at the table, his weight sinking into the chair so heavily that it scraped noisily against the hardwood floor. Alden stood quietly for a moment, then sat across from him and asked, "What happened with the car?"

Doug shrugged. "I don't know. I fell asleep and I didn't see it again after I woke up."

"Are you sleeping any better? Any more?"

Doug shook his head.

"Still the girl?" Alden asked.

"Yeah. I have nightmares."

Alden set his forearms on the table. "You know you had nothing to do with that. I made the decision. You know that, right?"

"It never would've happened," Doug said, "if we hadn't done what we did."

"You think it was all a mistake?"

"If it ended up killing her, then yeah, it was. You don't think it was a mistake? We killed that girl for nothing."

We killed her for Mark, Alden thought, but he couldn't say that to Doug. Jennifer hadn't been involved in Mark's death, but killing her had been a necessary part of avenging their friend, even if it was just a matter of circumstance.

"It's over now," Alden said. "Nothing can change what happened, but it's over now. We have to move past it."

Doug slammed his fist on the table so hard that Alden started in his chair.

"Jesus," Alden breathed.

"How?" Doug shouted. "How am I supposed to move past it?"

Alden took a deep breath and said, "Bad things happen, but you didn't have a part in this one. I know you think you did, but you didn't. We could've handled it differently. Maybe we would have if we'd had time to talk it over, but I made a decision in the moment. Do you understand that? I made the decision and I pulled the trigger."

Doug sat back and looked like he might vomit. "You say that like you don't even regret it."

"I don't," Alden said flatly. "Not anymore. I've settled it with myself. I know what I did and I know it was wrong, but I also know it was necessary. The circumstances required something that we weren't prepared to do. I did it. You didn't. Maybe that means you're a better person than me, and if so, so what? What does it matter? She's dead and we can't bring her back. I killed an innocent girl, but we balanced things out, right? We balanced things out for Mark."

"Yeah?" Doug sneered. "Well, who's going to balance things out for that girl?"

Alden clenched his teeth and shrugged one shoulder as a tingle of annoyance shot through his nerves.

Doug shook his head slowly, then shuddered violently and looked at the ceiling, his eyes suddenly overwhelmed by tears. He sucked in a sharp breath and held it, frozen for a few seconds before wailing, "What the fuck did we do?"

Alden looked at him with dull eyes. What could convince him to let it go? Was he capable of letting it go? No, Alden thought, he wasn't ready yet. Doug needed to cling to the pain. He felt he deserved it. He was hoping that the suffering would bring absolution, but how much punishment would be enough? How would he know?

"What's that look for?" Doug whimpered.

"Just thinking."

"How did you get over it?"

"I don't know," Alden said. "I broke down that night, but by the time I was leaving for the bar, I felt better. I don't really know why. I guess it was just perspective, you know? What happened was horrible, but it had to happen or we'd be headed for trial or worse by now."

"You didn't have to kill her. We could've let her go."

"No," Alden said. "If we'd let her go after killing him, she'd have gone to the police. Even if we'd let her go before killing him, once she found out, don't you think she might've put it together and reported us?"

"She had that stolen shit."

"Yeah, but that's not much in the face of a murder."

"I just don't know what to do."

Alden nodded and ran a hand over his face. "Is there anything I can do to help? Anything?"

Doug was quiet for a while, then said, "I don't think so."

"If there is," Alden said, "let me know."

"You taking off?"

"Unless you want me to hang around."

"No," Doug said, "that's okay."

Alden stood and walked to the door. Doug watched him from his chair, eyes still bloodshot and full of tears. He got up and walked slowly into the hall when Alden opened the door.

"Hey," Alden called, "you sure there's nothing I can do?"

"Yeah," was the weak, muffled reply.

Alden stepped outside and shut the door behind him.

He stopped at a gas station on the way home—just a little service station on a stretch of country road. There was an old, distressed payphone near the door. Alden took a handful of change from his console and got out of the car. There was only one customer at the pumps and traffic on the road was light.

He picked up the receiver and dropped several coins into the slot. He glanced again at the customer at the pumps, then took the piece of paper from his pocket and dialed the number there.

A high pitched tone sounded and a recording told him the number had been disconnected. He sighed and hung up, then went back to his car. He'd have to find another way to get what he wanted.

A few minutes on the computer led him to a website based in Canada that claimed to sell American novelty identification that could match the real thing. Alden clicked on several sample pictures from various states, but he didn't know how accurate they might be. He checked the sample image from Vermont and compared it to his own driver's license. It looked like a perfect match.

There was a link to an order form, but there was no way to submit it online. He had to print a hard copy and fill it out. There were instructions in bold that exclaimed, *Do not write "driver's license" anywhere on this document!*

Alden smirked, tore off the warning above the dotted line, and picked up a pen. He almost wrote his own name. He paused, then took a phone book from one of his desk drawers and opened it to a random page. He let his finger fall onto the paper and looked at the name there.

"Tourant," Alden said appreciatively. "Okay."

He wrote the last name on the form, then paused again. He thought for a moment about what first name he'd like. "Marcus," he decided. That was fitting. He filled out the rest with a fake address in Vermont and signed the alias on a line at the bottom.

He took an envelope from his desk and wrote the Canadian address on it, then took ninety dollars from his pocket and folded the form around the cash. He slipped the paper into the envelope and looked around the room. He needed to include a photograph.

The sample picture showed a blue background and he didn't have any way to recreate that. Instead, he used his digital camera to take a picture of his own license. He copied the image from the camera to his computer, then used an image editing program to crop it and clean it up a bit. It wasn't perfect, but it would work. He printed the color image and put it in the envelope with the form and the cash.

Alden spent the following morning in front of his computer again with a cup of coffee and a pair of buttered waffles. Outside, the sun was alone in a clear sky and Alden left the office window open to let in some fresh air. The guttural growl of a lawn mower drifted on the slight breeze.

He scrolled through a list of available jobs with one hand and ate a waffle with the other. His qualifications didn't allow for many options, but even those positions out of reach didn't excite him. He looked at the screen and felt his stomach tighten as boredom turned to frustration.

I.T. Specialist. Human Resources Manager. Retail Management Trainee. Software Programmer. Who would ever be happy doing these things? He returned to the site's main page and expanded his search nationwide, but found more of the same. He sighed and ate the other waffle while the sound of the lawnmower undulated back and forth across a plot of grass somewhere down the street.

"Oh, fuck it," he said to himself.

He scrolled halfway down the list and clicked on an opening for a management position in a retail store. He didn't know until the page loaded that they sold pet products. He didn't like animals much, but some dogs were all right, he supposed. He clicked on the purple button at the bottom of the page and sent his resume.

He returned to his search and scrolled to a few more places in the long list of jobs. He didn't look at the locations as he applied for several more positions, though he did notice that one was in Hawaii. That might be an interesting change, he thought, but weren't their gun laws strict? Well, it wasn't like he hadn't broken those kinds of laws before. He smirked.

He took his coffee in hand and sat back. He took a sip and thought about Jennifer. He remembered the way she'd spoken and moved. He remembered her eyes, alive and dead. He tried to be moved. His mind yearned for his heart to ache or his eyes to cry, but no reaction came. He breathed a short, confused snort. What the hell was wrong with him?

He thought about the way Tom had died, writhing desperately as his blood sprayed from the wound in his neck. Again, he felt no discomfort. There was a benign sense of pleasure instead. He took another sip of coffee and his mind drifted to the bag of money in the locker at the gym. How much was in there? How much time had he spent working out the details on Tom? What, exactly, was the return for his effort? Probably more than what a retail manager or a software programmer would make in that time, but they didn't have to worry about life in prison.

Pedro had been a mistake. There had been no preparation. They never knew what they were coming up against. Maybe they should've sat on the hotel for a while. Maybe that would've given Jennifer time to get out, but it didn't matter. They hadn't sat on the hotel and she hadn't had time to get out. What happened, happened.

He finished his coffee and brought the cup into the kitchen with the plate of waffle crumbs. He washed them in the sink and set them to dry. The street outside was bright with sunlight and he strained to see his car in the shadows under the covered parking space across the way.

His cell phone rang, but the warbling tone was muffled. He turned around and wondered for a few seconds where he'd left it, then trotted upstairs to his bedroom. It was still charging next to his bed. He unplugged it and looked at the screen. Doug.

"Hey," he answered.

There was quiet sobbing and loud breathing on the other end. Alden waited a moment, then asked, "What's going on?"

A long pause, another sob, more heavy breathing, then, "I'm going to turn myself in."

Alden's hands went numb and he nearly dropped the phone. A surge of adrenaline made his limbs shaky and he sat on the bed. "Have you called anyone yet? The police?"

"Not yet," Doug slurred.

"Don't call yet," Alden said. "I'll be right over, okay?"

"Yeah, yeah. Okay."

"I'll be right over. Wait for me."

"Okay."

Alden closed his phone and put it in the holder on his nightstand, then attached it to his belt. He went downstairs and picked up his keys from the kitchen counter, then stopped. What was he doing? He needed to think about this, but there was no time to think and there was no way to know what Doug might do. Alden growled and walked into the living room. He took the small book from the coffee table and looked at the drawing of the man in the yellow suit on the cover.

He wanted to get to Doug's house as quickly as possible, but he resisted the urge to speed and obeyed the limits. He parked behind Doug's SUV and got out. He slammed the car door and walked with long, fast strides to the front door. It was open. Alden entered and shut the door behind him.

Doug was sitting at the kitchen table, his head in his hands. He didn't look up when Alden took the chair from the other side of the table and brought it around to the side. He sat, only a corner of dark wood separating him from his friend.

"Talk to me," Alden said softly. "What's going on?"

"I can't take it," Doug said, not looking up.

"You can't go to the police."

"I have to go," Doug groaned, meeting Alden's eyes. "I have to turn myself in. I can't take this anymore."

"You want to go to prison?" Alden asked. "You want me to go to prison? You can't go to the police."

"I won't tell them about you."

"Yes," Alden said, "you will. These people get information out of people who don't want to give it for a living. You'll tell them about me even though you don't want to. You can't go to the police."

"I have to," Doug said, shaking his head methodically. "I have to."

Alden rubbed his hands over his lips, then said, "We had a deal. We were in this together."

"Like with the girl?" Doug asked harshly.

"Are you drunk? Vicodin?"

"Fuck you."

Alden sighed. "Don't do this to yourself."

"I have to."

"No, you don't. Listen to me. Give it time, okay? Just give it a little more time. It's only been a few days. Give it time."

Doug shook his head wildly. "I can't. I can't do it."

"Talk to me, at least. What's going on? Why do you want to turn yourself in?"

"The girl," Doug said, sobbing. "Oh, that goddamn girl. We should've left, you know? We should've just left. She's fuckin' dead! God, she's fuckin' dead." He sobbed again. "I can't do this anymore. I have to tell somebody. I have to make it right somehow."

"So you're going to turn yourself in to make it right for her?"

Doug nodded.

"I killed her," Alden said. "It was me, not you. How is it going to make anything right if they punish you?"

"It will," Doug said, sniffing and sitting straighter. "I just know it will."

"You don't know that. You think that. You want that, but you don't know it. Turning yourself in won't accomplish anything and it'll put me in prison, too. You'll talk about me, Doug."

"I'd never do that."

"You would," Alden said. "That's something I just know."

"I'd never."

Alden wanted to slam his fist on the table and scream, but he didn't. He sat back in the chair and looked at his friend, weary and confused. He watched Doug tangle his fingers in his red hair and wondered how he could get some sort of control.

"Do you want more death?" Alden asked.

"What? No. Fuck, no!"

"Then you can't go to the police. If you go away, I go away. You'll talk about me and I'll be in prison for the rest of my life. That's as good as dead. It might really be dead if it got out that I was a cop, and that sort of thing doesn't stay quiet."

"I won't talk about you!" Doug shouted.

Alden shook his head and said, "You don't know that."

"I have to do this."

"It won't bring her back, you know."

"I know that."

"What is it you think this will accomplish, then?" Alden asked. "I don't think it's about the girl at all. I think it's about you."

"What? Come on!"

Alden shook his head again. "It's about you. It's about you making yourself feel better. You care about the girl, I know that, but that's not what this is really about. It won't change anything for her, but you think it would change everything for you."

"That's not true."

"I've known you my whole life," Alden said softly. "There's no shame in looking out for yourself, but think about what you're doing. Isn't that what we've been trying for through all this? We needed to think of everything—all the effects, now and later. Look at the totality of this. If you turn yourself in, you're turning me in. You're killing me."

Doug put his head in his hands and mumbled, "I know what'll happen if I turn myself in. I have no idea what'll happen if I don't. I'll just go crazy or something. This is driving me crazy. I can't do it."

Alden rubbed his eyes. How could he change Doug's mind? There was no point arguing with him. He was at a point where conversation wouldn't change his opinion. He needed something to jar him out of the corner into which he'd backed himself. He thought it was difficult to live with what they'd done, but did he know how difficult it would be to do what he wanted to do now?

"Listen," Alden said, "I trust you. If you tell me something, I'll believe it, okay? Do you swear you'll never say a word about me?"

"Yeah," Doug said, almost whining. "Yes."

Alden leaned on the table and nodded. "Okay. Get some paper and a pen. If you really want to do it this way, we need to make sure you have your story straight. You'll need to lie like your life depends on it, because mine will, understand? We'll outline a statement and you'll have to commit it to memory. You'll have to know every little detail."

Doug stood listlessly and walked into the hallway. He came back a moment later, a yellow legal pad and a blue pen in his hands. He set them on the table and sat down again.

"Basically," Alden said, "we have to go back through everything and just take me out. You'll have to tell them that you did everything. You researched it, you planned it, and you pulled it off."

"Okay," Doug said.

"You'll need to tell them you killed Jennifer," Alden told him.

The name produced a reaction. Doug's eyes widened momentarily and he shook his head once, then took a deep breath and nodded.

Alden held back a grimace and said, "You'll need to have your thoughts organized, so let's start." He pointed to the paper. "Write it like a story, but with me taken out. You'll have to include everything you did, like buying the supplies, and take credit for everything I did, like putting together the suppressor and following Tom. When you're done, we'll go over it and clean it up. Then you'll have to commit it to memory."

He watched Doug write for almost half an hour. His hands were shaking and the script was sloppy, but Alden could read it from where he sat. He felt restless waiting for each word. It was like listening to a child try to read.

"Okay," Doug said when he was done.

Alden nodded and forced a smile. It wasn't working the way he'd intended. Doug was clearly unsettled by the statement, but it wasn't enough to scare him off. What the hell was it going to take?

"What now?" Doug asked.

"Bathroom first."

Alden stood and walked into the hallway. The bathroom was halfway down on the right. He went inside and used the toilet, then washed his hands and looked at himself in the mirror. He couldn't let Doug go the police. He didn't want to see his friend spend the rest of his life in prison and he wasn't convinced Doug could keep his story straight in his present condition. How the hell was he going to turn this around? He needed to make a bigger impact. He needed a stronger way to make his point.

Doug was threatening their lives. Didn't he understand that? They might as well have had guns to their heads. Alden examined his reflection and shot himself a wry smile. Fuck it, he thought. Doug was the only friend he had left. He wasn't going to let that end.

He left the bathroom, but didn't go to the kitchen. He went instead to Doug's bedroom. The pile of clothes in the corner was larger and messier than it had been before. The closet door was open and Doug's Kimber was sitting on the shelf. Alden took it down. The hammer was back and the safety was engaged. He thumbed the safety off and pulled the slide back slightly, finding a round in the chamber. He let go of the slide and reengaged the safety, then carried the gun back to the kitchen.

Doug had his head on the table. Alden sat and Doug looked up, rubbed his face, and asked quietly, "What next?"

Alden reached across the corner of the table and grabbed Doug's right wrist. He tightened his grip and Doug dropped the pen. Alden flipped the gun around under the table, then pushed the grip into the Doug's hand.

"You want to do this?" Alden shouted.

Doug's eyes were wide and his mouth opened and closed rapidly. Alden pushed the gun harder into Doug's hand and forced his finger inside the trigger guard, making sure his own index finger was wedged beneath the safety lever, preventing it from being disengaged.

"What are you doing?" Doug asked in a panic.

"You're hurting," Alden seethed, "because you think that girl's dead because of you. You turn yourself in, you're killing me. Understand? So if you want to fucking kill me, do it!"

"No!" Doug screamed, trying to pull away.

Alden pulled hard, bringing the muzzle of the pistol against his throat, then wrestling Doug's arm higher and putting the muzzle to his head.

"Stop!" Doug cried, feet scraping across the uneven hardwood floor.

"Do it!" Alden barked. "Pull the trigger and kill me! That's what you want, right? Turning yourself in is killing me, so just fucking do it already!"

Doug's voice was high and frantic. "What are you doing?"

"It's what you're doing! You're sending me to prison. You're killing me, understand? Is this what you want?"

"No! Fuck!"

"Then don't turn yourself in! You do it, you kill me. So if you're going to turn yourself in, just pull the goddamn trigger now!"

Doug's face, already wet with tears, twisted in horror and he shook his head violently. He jaw clenched hard and blood appeared on his lips. The motion of his head quickly took over his body and great sobs made the muscles in his limbs tighten, then go slack.

Alden's heart skipped and then ached. He felt it drop as if a weak foundation had given way. It plunged downward into his chest and for an instant he was confused, but looking into Doug's eyes, he understood. Doug couldn't be convinced. He was beyond intractable. It was hopeless. It didn't matter what happened. He was going to turn himself in and they were both going to end up in prison for the rest of their lives.

Alden's heart stopped tumbling and started burning. The heat spread rapidly through his insides. There was fear in Doug's eyes. He, Alden, was the cause. Doug was frightened by him. As he should be, Alden thought, because he wouldn't go to prison; he'd rather be dead than caged. Alden had put the gun in his friend's hand, but Doug wouldn't pull the trigger and he wouldn't change his mind. It left Alden with no options. Doug had already set the course. Only one of them would leave this kitchen.

Doug's terrified weeping had overcome him. Alden felt the weakness that followed. He felt the weight of Doug's arm as it went limp. His left hand still held Doug's and his left index finger was still beneath the safety lever. He used his right hand to grip the inside of Doug's elbow and he stood abruptly. He rotated Doug's forearm, removing the muzzle from his own head and placing it in line with this friend's.

Doug responded, his muscles tightening again as he reacted instinctively to the aggressive motion. Alden was faster. His right hand moved from Doug's elbow to the gun as the finger of his left hand moved from below the safety lever to above it; it clicked downward. Alden put his own finger over Doug's inside the trigger guard and he pressed it back.

The gun fired. The bullet struck Doug above the right temple at a sharp angle. Alden felt blood and tissue spray across his neck and chin, wet and hot. He watched Doug fall out of the chair onto the kitchen floor, but he didn't hear it. His ears were overwhelmed with high-pitched ringing.

Doug's left leg jerked spasmodically. Alden watched it for a few seconds. His heart was pounding and he could feel the pressure inside his ears, but there was no sound. It made him dizzy.

Move, he told himself. He blinked and went to the kitchen window. He looked outside without touching the curtains. A car went by on the road, but there was no one in sight and the neighbors were a mile away or more. He looked back at Doug's body. Blood was spreading from the wound in his head and seeping from his nose. Alden went to the body and picked up the gun.

The slide was slightly to the rear. The next round had failed to feed properly, having been jammed upward into the top of the chamber. Alden took the gun to the kitchen sink and grabbed a dish towel, then put the towel down. It would probably have residue on it from the dish soap. He took a clean towel from a drawer instead and wiped the gun thoroughly.

He carried it in the cloth to Doug's body and placed it in his friend's dead hand. He carefully moved Doug's fingers around the grip and pressed hard. He took Doug's index finger and pressed it onto the trigger—there was no risk of discharging the jammed round with the slide out of battery. When he was satisfied, he let go and the weight of the pistol came to rest on the floor, stretching Doug's limp fingers.

Alden looked down at his shirt. Blood had splattered across it. He wiped his face and hands with the towel, then walked around the table and took the cloth by the sink. He might've gotten blood on it when he'd picked it up the first time.

Doug's cell phone was on the counter by the coffee maker. Alden carefully took the pen on the table by its cap and used it to navigate the phone's menu, deleting the record of Doug's earlier call. He waited for the small screen to dim before wiping the pen's cap with the cloth and returning it to the table.

He went to the front door and turned to look at the scene. Doug's leg was still moving slightly, but his wide, lifeless eyes were staring at the ceiling. Blood had made a dark, imperfect halo around his head.

Alden turned and left the house. He went to his car and took the small "technical manual" from the seat. He brought it back into the house and felt his stomach churn; the blood had spread and the wound was wide enough to allow Alden a glimpse of brain matter. He felt vomit touch the back of his throat and he closed his teary eyes.

"Jesus," he whispered.

He dropped the book on the table and rushed outside.

VII

His heart was still beating fast, but there was no ache in it. He drove carefully, watching his speedometer. There was a gas station on the side of the country road—the same one from which he'd tried to call for the fake ID—but he didn't dare stop to dispose of the towels. His shirt was still speckled with blood and he didn't want to be noticed.

He checked the rearview mirror and saw no cars there. He was breathing slowly and deeply, trying to keep his heart rate down. His ears were still ringing from the gunshot.

Doug had been just like Pedro and Tom. He hadn't known what was going to happen until the very last moment. Maybe he was even more surprised. At least Tom and Pedro had understood the possibility of death at the end of their ordeals.

For the similarity to the others, even the superiority, Alden hadn't felt the same sense of intoxicating power. He still didn't feel much of anything—not yet. He was probably too shocked to have any significant reaction. It had happened fast and he couldn't really process the sequence of events. He remembered what had happened, but he was having a hard time putting it in order in his head. He'd nearly forgotten to leave the book behind.

He passed the gas station and looked at the two towels on the floor in front of the passenger seat. He'd have to throw away the mat, too.

"Fuck!" he spat.

The book he'd left on the table. It still had his fingerprints on it. How had he forgotten that? He growled and slowed the car, pulling over to the shoulder. He checked his mirrors and the road ahead, then turned around and sped back toward Doug's house. He ignored the speed limits.

He parked behind Doug's SUV again and left the car running as he rushed into the house. He didn't look at the body. He took another clean dish towel from the drawer and used it to wipe the outside of the book. He took a deep breath and tried to swallow, but his mouth was dry.

He knelt over Doug's corpse and took his left hand, pressing it against the book in several places. Then he moved the gun and took prints from the right hand as well. As he replaced the weapon, he couldn't help but look at the dead face, eyes still wide from the fright that had preceded the end. Alden used the towel to put the book back on the table, then took the cloth with him back to his car. He threw it on the floor with the others and drove away.

He stripped off his clothes and left them on the bathroom floor while he showered. The water was hot and he washed himself quickly, scrubbing his face, neck, and hands with extra vigor. After drying off, he went to his bedroom and put on a new set of clothes.

He went downstairs to the kitchen for two trash bags. He used one to pick up the towels, mat, and clothes, and shoved everything into the second bag. He carried it downstairs and set it by the door, then went back to his bedroom. He took a small plastic bin of cleaning supplies from the closet and brought it to the bathroom. He sprayed a thick layer of cleaner on the floor and scrubbed it with an old rag. When he was finished, he returned the bin to the closet and carried the rag downstairs where he added it to the trash bag. He washed his hands in the kitchen sink and almost put on his shoes.

He looked at them for a moment. The brown leather was worn and comfortable. He'd bought them a long time ago—years. They were good shoes, but he picked them up and threw them into the trash bag, too. With a sigh, he went back to the bedroom and brought the bin of cleaning supplies downstairs. He used paper towels to wipe the cleaner over the tile inside the door where his shoes had been, then threw them into the bag on top of the old leather. He replaced the bin again and came back to the black trash bag. He stared at it for a moment before tying it and putting on a pair of sneakers.

He carried the trash bag outside and put it in the trunk of his car, then drove a few miles away to a strip mall beside a busy thoroughfare. He found three red dumpsters around the back and threw away the trash bag in the closest one. He looked around before getting into his car, but saw no one else behind the buildings. He was careful pulling out into traffic.

Then he went home to wait. The sun was high and bright when he parked his car across from the townhouse. The air was hot and thick. It had to be over ninety degrees and his face was slippery with sweat by the time he was inside. He kicked off his sneakers and went to the living room. He turned on the air conditioner and stood there, staring out at the overgrown, sun-bleached lawn.

He felt tired. He thought about taking a nap and walked upstairs, but his bedroom was bright and his bed looked uninviting. He felt guilty for wanting to sleep and went to the bathroom where the light was dulled by the blinds. He looked at his reflection and his heart began to pound.

A loaded gun had been pressed against that head. Alden reached up and touched the spot, just above his nose and a little to the left. He could've died. His finger could've slipped from beneath the safety lever.

"Jesus," he said. "What the fuck?"

He put his hands on the edge of the sink and leaned forward, staring himself in the eyes. He clenched his teeth and squinted.

"That's it," he told himself. "Nothing else left. No one else, now. Just you. Isn't that just fucking great? Isn't that just what you deserved?"

He turned on the sink and washed his hands and face with cold water, then went back to the living room where he sat on the couch and stared at the blank television screen.

The call came just after nine o'clock at night. He didn't recognize the number, but it was a local cell phone. He took a deep breath and answered, trying hard to sound inquisitive when he asked, "Hello?"

"Al," said a quiet voice in high tones.

"Who's calling?"

"It's Tiffany, Al."

"Oh, hey. What's up?"

He heard her wail on the other end of the line, then sniff and cough and wail again. After several long seconds, she said, "He's dead."

Alden tried to sound confused. "What are you talking about?"

"Doug," Tiffany said. "Doug's dead. He's dead. Oh, God!"

"What?" Alden asked, feinting alarm. "What are you talking about?"

"He, God, he—"

"Slow down. What happened?"

"He's dead," she shuddered.

"Where are you?"

"The hospital. The emergency room."

"I'll be right there."

The first thing he noticed was the green, unmarked police cruiser in the parking lot, just outside the doors to the ER. He felt his lungs start to burn and he had to breathe harder to accommodate his rushing blood. He told himself to stay calm. There were countless reasons a police officer would be at the emergency room, but no, that was probably wishful thinking.

He parked and got out of the car. It was hot, but not quite as humid as it had been in the afternoon. Alden walked through the sliding glass doors and into the waiting area. He saw Tiffany sitting on the right, her face in her hands and concealed by her auburn hair. Doug's mother and father sat beside her, holding each other and crying. He'd looked more like his father, Alden thought.

There was a man in a shirt and tie standing beyond them, looking thoughtful. A gold badge was clipped to his belt and a pistol was holstered on his left hip. Alden tried to ignore him and sat next to Tiffany. She looked up, her eyes red and swollen, then resumed crying. Alden looked over her at Doug's father, stout and red-haired like his son had been.

"What happened?" Alden asked.

"He died," Doug's father said hoarsely.

The man with the badge stepped over and said, "I'm sorry, but are you Alden?"

"Yeah."

"I was hoping we could talk for a moment."

"What happened?"

"We can talk about that. My name's Peter Cary. I'm a detective with the State Police. Can we step outside?"

Alden looked between Tiffany and Doug's parents, then stood and walked outside. As the doors slid shut, he asked again, "What happened?"

"Miss Warren said that you were good friends with Doug. I'm sorry to tell you that it appears that he took his own life earlier today."

Alden gave the detective a blank stare and asked flatly, "What?"

"I'm sorry."

"What?" Alden asked again, raising his voice. "How? What happened? He wouldn't do that!"

Cary patted the air. "Miss Warren said that he'd been depressed lately. Do you think that was true?"

Alden narrowed his eyes. He used the anger to gain time. He didn't know how to act here. What was this detective after? Was he really trying to substantiate information or did he suspect foul play? There must have been signs. The spatter from the wound would probably indicate that someone else had been there. They probably knew it wasn't suicide. The gun, at least, couldn't have been clean, could it? They would probably be able to tell where the other person had been standing.

Alden twisted his neck slightly to the side and said, "You just told me my best friend killed himself and you're going to ask me if he was depressed? What the hell do you think? He was just whistling a fucking tune and, 'Oh, I think I'll kill myself now?' Come on. Christ!"

"I'm sorry," Cary said. "I just wanted your opinion."

Alden breathed hard through his nose and looked at the dark sky, then returned his eyes to the detective and said, "He was upset. He wouldn't talk to me about it."

"Do you remember when you first noticed he was upset?"

Alden ran a hand through his hair and paced. "I don't know," he said. "We went out for a drink one night and he was upset. He wouldn't tell me what it was about."

"Do you remember when you went out? What day?"

"Last Sunday. We always go out on Sundays."

"And did you see him after that?"

"Yeah. Once."

"When was that?"

"Yesterday."

"Where did you meet him yesterday?"

"At his place," Alden said, continuing to pace. "What happened? I mean, what did he do?"

"What do you mean?"

"What did he do? How did he do it?"

Cary seemed interested by the question. That wasn't good. Alden wanted to say something else, but that probably wouldn't help. If anything, it would likely arouse more suspicion.

"It was a gunshot wound," Cary said.

Alden sighed and stopped pacing. He put his hands on his hips and looked at the pavement. The pavement. He thought back to the night Mark had died. He'd collapsed to the pavement.

"Fuck," Alden said quietly, and after a moment, he knelt, then sat on the cracked parking lot.

Cary knelt and said, "I'm sorry. When you went to his place, what did you talk about?"

Alden's heart was racing again. He could feel his face flushing. Would it be noticed? Would it be taken as a normal response or something indicative of deception?

"Alden?"

"Sorry," Alden said. "I'm sorry. This is just, it's just, you know, a lot to take in right now."

"I know. Do you remember what you talked about yesterday?"

"He called me. He was upset and I told him I'd stop by. I got there and he didn't want to talk about anything. He just kept telling me not to worry about it, so I left." Alden shook his head and grabbed his hair. "Jesus, I should've stayed."

"The Sunday when you met for drinks," Cary said. "Do you remember what time it was?"

"Around ten, I think. It was usually ten."

"Did Doug work that day?"

"I don't know," Alden said. "He worked nights. He never really got the same ones off all the time."

"How was he before that night? Did you notice anything unusual about his behavior?"

"I don't think so."

"Did he mention anything about traveling?"

"What?" Alden asked, holding his palms up in mock confusion.

"About traveling—being away?"

"No," Alden said. "I don't think so."

Cary stood up and offered Alden a hand. He grabbed it and got back to his feet. The detective took a long breath and said, "Miss Warren said you used to be a cop."

"Deputy."

"I remember the shooting," Cary said, nodding thoughtfully. "A friend of mine helped with the investigation."

Alden looked away toward the hospital doors.

"You did well," Cary said, "and you got screwed, but they said you took it all and didn't even blink. Never complained."

Alden nodded again and looked at the cracked pavement between his feet, wondering where this conversation was going. What was this about? Was he trying to develop rapport through camaraderie?

"This is a tough thing," Cary went on, "but you'll get through it. You're a tough kid. Just hang in there."

"I'll try," Alden told him. "I'm trying."

"I might need to talk to you some more."

"Yeah," Alden said. "You need my number?"

"Sure."

Alden gave it to him and he wrote it in a small notepad along with Alden's name, address, and date of birth. He closed the pad and put it in the back pocket of his trousers.

"Let's go back inside," the detective said. "I think your friend's family would like to have you there."

Alden followed Cary inside and took the seat next to Tiffany. She was still crying and she turned toward him. He put a hand on her shoulder and she grabbed his shirt and shoved her face into his chest, weeping loudly with shaking shoulders. Doug's father rubbed her back while his mother sat silently, staring at the swinging doors that led deeper into the hospital. Her son's body was back there somewhere, tagged and stored and awaiting an autopsy.

Alden looked over Tiffany and said to Doug's father, "I'm so sorry. If there's anything I can do, please, just say so."

His father smiled and said, "Thanks, Al."

"You were always there for him," his mother said, coming out of her reverie and turning toward them. "You were always there for him and for Mark. They were lucky to have you."

Alden forced a smile and felt his eyes start to sting as tears blurred his vision. He blinked them away and pulled Tiffany closer. He stayed silent, but his mind was rushing wildly, trying to put the pieces together and make some sense of the day. He'd stolen love from a beautiful soul and he'd torn a family apart. *Dear God,* he thought, *what have I done?*

He stopped at a liquor store on the way home and bought a bottle of cheap rum. He threw the paper bag away in a trash bin on his way out and drove home in a daze. He twisted off the cap between his car and the front door and took a large drink before going inside.

He didn't bother with the lights. He went to the kitchen and took a glass down from the cupboard, then filled it with rum. He capped the bottle and left it on the counter. He thought about sitting down in the living room, but drank the glass of rum over the sink instead. It only took a few seconds for the golden liquor to disappear.

He grimaced and set the glass in the sink, then walked with a slow, aimless gait up the stairs to his bedroom. He plugged his cell phone into its charger and undressed, letting his clothes fall in a pile on the floor.

He slid under the covers and stared at the ceiling. His thoughts drifted, always unfocused. He thought about Doug, but he only saw fragments of old memories in his mind's eye. Laughing about the camouflage hat. Kayaking on the lake. Dinner at a cheap restaurant downtown. The orange light from the setting sun the day they brought Mark to Tom's house.

He breathed in a deep breath and let out a long, loud groan. He turned his head and looked at the empty side of his bed. How long had he been alone? It didn't matter, he thought. He hadn't really been alone, anyway. There had been friends to distract him, but that was over.

Now he was alone.

The following morning, he called the real estate agent through which he'd purchased his townhouse. He told him that he was looking to sell as soon as possible.

"When will you be ready to show it?" the realtor asked.

"Right now. I'm taking a few things with me, but I have to move soon. I'd like to sell it as is. I have a new job lined up and I have to be there to get started."

"We can certainly arrange that."

"Thanks. I'll call you later and we can work out the details."

He hung up and went to his computer. Two of the jobs for which he'd applied had sent replies. They were interested in hiring him immediately, provided he was willing to relocate and made a good impression during a phone interview. Neither of them offered compensation for the move, but that wasn't much trouble. There was a duffel bag full of cash waiting to be spent just a few minutes away.

He got a call an hour later from Doug's father.

"Al," he said, "I just wanted to let you know the wake will be on Sunday. Ten o'clock at the funeral home on Shelburne Road."

"I know it. Thanks for telling me."

"Of course. He'd want you there more than anyone else."

"Thanks."

"You hear that bullshit they're saying?"

"No. What do you mean?"

Doug's father huffed and said, "Police say he wrote a note. They say he killed that boy in the North End and those two in Plattsburgh."

"What?" Alden asked. "That can't be true."

"They say they can figure it. It was in the paper. Supporting evidence and a bunch of other bullshit, but my boy wasn't no murderer."

"I know," Alden said quietly, almost whispering.

"Don't believe it, Al, you hear me?"

"I don't. Never would. I knew Doug. He'd never do something like that—never in his life."

"It's just bullshit, telling us these things, putting it in the damn paper for everyone to read."

"I know."

Doug's father was breathing heavily, but Alden could hear him trying to control himself until he managed to say, "You stay well, all right? We'll see you on Sunday."

"You, too," Alden replied. "I'll see you then."

He hung up and set his phone on the kitchen counter. More than anyone else? It almost made him laugh, but the sharp ache in his chest stopped him and took the strength from his legs. He collapsed against the refrigerator and sat on the linoleum, staring up at the window.

What was wrong with him? He should've been contemplating suicide himself after what he'd done. He'd murdered his only friend. His lifelong friend was dead and the blood was on his hands. He deserved more punishment than an hour's heartache a few times a day.

It had been necessary. He understood that. If it hadn't happened the way it had happened, he'd be in custody and awaiting trial for three homicides. That was something he wasn't willing to do, but he'd crossed so far over such a clear line. He'd done a terrible thing—something far worse than killing an innocent girl to prevent her from being a witness. She'd been a stranger. Doug had been his friend—his lifelong friend and the only one left. He'd destroyed something irreplaceable.

. . .

He slept until late afternoon the next day. He felt groggy despite the long sleep and getting out of bed made his muscles ache. His back hurt and his ribs were sore; he felt like he'd been in a fight. He dragged his feet to the bathroom and took a shower. The hot water felt good, but did nothing to relieve the pain. He couldn't relax and his shoulders felt cramped. He left his discarded underwear on the bathroom floor and walked naked to his bedroom. He dressed and went downstairs.

He opened the refrigerator, but he felt no desire to eat. He looked outside and saw a few clouds scattered across the blue sky. Why wasn't it dark and raining? It should've been dark and raining. It didn't feel right to be able to see the sun. It was the same sense of incongruity he'd felt seeing Mark's casket hovering over the open ground.

He went back to his bedroom and took his cell phone from the charger on the nightstand. He scrolled through his recent calls and dialed the realtor.

"Green Mountain North Realtors," a feminine voice answered.

"Hi," Alden croaked, "I'm calling for Pat."

"I'm sorry. He's out of the office at the moment."

"That's okay. Can I speak with someone else?"

"Sure. May I ask what it's regarding?"

"I'm looking to put my home on the market as soon as possible."

"One moment."

There was a click followed by several seconds of silence. Then he heard the sound of a receiver being lifted and another woman's voice said politely, "This is Suzanne."

"Hi, my name's Alden. I spoke with Pat yesterday about putting my townhouse up for sale on short notice."

"Alden, yes, Pat told me. I think we met when you bought your place a couple years ago."

"I think so."

"Have you had a recent appraisal?"

"No," Alden said. "I need to leave very soon. I was hoping you might be able to arrange the details for me. Sorry for the tight timetable. I'll be out of the area in the next few days."

"Okay," she said, sounding unsure.

"Could I drop off the house papers and a key, maybe?"

"That would be fine. We'll have a few things you'll need to sign."

"It's no problem. Can I come by today?"

"That would be fine."

"I'll be there a in a bit."

The realtors' office was on the second floor of a small commercial building in a large commercial park. It was bland—white walls and gray carpet beneath desks made of fake wood. Alden was greeted by a young Asian woman in a yellow blouse. He tried to return her smile, but he didn't think he did well.

"I'm here to see Suzanne," he said. "I'm Alden."

She led him down a short hallway to a door on the right. It was open and she knocked on the frame, then motioned for Alden to enter.

"Hi, Alden," said a tall, dark-haired woman behind the desk inside.

"Hi."

She stood and came forward to shake his hand, saying, "Nice to see you again."

"You, too."

He held out a manila folder and she took it.

"That should be everything," he told her. "The extra key's taped inside. I'll be out in a few days—Tuesday at the latest."

"Okay, great. I just have a few things to go over with you."

She had a neat stack of papers on the corner of her desk and she went through them with him one by one. He didn't really care to listen. He nodded and smiled when she smiled and signed where she pointed. It couldn't have taken more than twenty minutes, he thought.

"We'll let you know when it's appraised and on the market," she told him with a smile. "We will need you to return for the closing, unless there's someone with power of attorney. Congratulations on the new job."

"Thanks," Alden replied flatly. "I should be able to get back."

She handed him a business card and said, "Take care. Give us a call if you have any questions."

"Okay," he said.

She was still smiling when he left her office, but he could picture the smile disappearing as soon as he was in the hallway. The receptionist said, "Have a nice day!" on his way out, but he didn't reply.

He walked slowly to his car, eyes shifting between the asphalt and the sky. The clouds were thicker, but he could still see blue in places. He frowned, then scowled and spat, "Nice fucking day."

At home, he drank and packed. He unplugged his computer and sorted through the tangle of cables behind it. He hadn't written down the phone numbers for the companies interested in hiring him, but that didn't really matter. He didn't care if he got those jobs. He would look when he stopped moving—if he stopped moving.

It was just about motion. He wanted to be distracted. He didn't want to be around the places and things that made him think. He wanted to go someplace where he could be mindless—he wanted oblivion without the price of death.

Why didn't he want death? Wouldn't anyone else have welcomed it? Wouldn't anyone else have considered it justice? His crime was too great to be forgivable. He was certain about that. He and Doug had been like brothers. That made him little better than Cain, so why shouldn't he suffer the same fate?

He looked around the office and down at the jumble of cables around his feet. This place didn't feel like home, anyway.

. . .

The alarm clock woke him. It's buzzing made him angry and he nearly struck out at it with closed eyes, but he felt too nauseous to move that quickly. He fumbled with the switch instead, his chest burning and his head aching. Standing was difficult—his balance was mostly lost to the rum.

He took underwear from his bureau and took a shower. He didn't turn on the bathroom fan and breathed in the thick steam. It seemed to calm his stomach and ease the ache behind his eyes. When he was done, he put on the underwear and went to his closet. He hadn't thought about renting a suit for the wake or the funeral. He put on a black dress shirt and black slacks.

He went back to the bathroom and looked at himself in the mirror. A few days' stubble made his face look rough, but he didn't have time to shave. He took his cell phone from the bedroom and his keys from the kitchen, then put on uncomfortable black dress shoes and stepped into the sunlight.

It made his headache worse, but the air was cooler than usual and a few deep breaths took away the last of his nausea. His heart began to pound as he walked toward his car. He didn't want to go to the wake. He didn't want to face what he'd done, but there was no choice.

"No choice," he said to himself as he started the car.

He backed out and started for the funeral home. He checked his mirrors, looking for any cars that had pulled out of the small development behind him. Might he have left a partial fingerprint on the gun? The book?

"You're still deep in it," he reminded himself.

There were very few people at the wake. It had been kept private. Doug's family was clustered at the back of the room. Tiffany stood nearby with another woman unfamiliar to Alden. They looked similar. Maybe she was a sister or a more distant relative.

Doug's father noticed Alden first. He approached and they shook hands, then embraced. Alden gave him a few light pats on the back.

"Thanks for coming."

Alden didn't know what to say and began to feel awkward as the silence lengthened, but a renewed bout of weeping from Doug's mother drew his father away. Alden exchanged glances with Tiffany. She forced a feeble smile below teary eyes. He tried to smile back, but failed.

The coffin was at the back of the room, behind the cluster of family members. Alden approached slowly. Each step took agonizing effort. He wanted to close his eyes, but forced them open. His jaw clenched and he felt a scalding tightness in his throat. It was painful to swallow.

The casket was made of dark, polished wood and brushed brass. The lid was closed. Alden's nausea returned; he knew why the lid was closed and he knew what his friend looked like inside. Had they cleaned the blood from the kitchen floor?

Alden didn't realize he was still moving forward until his hand brushed the cold brass of the handle. He unwillingly took hold of the metal with one hand, then both. He stared down at the gleaming wood and was absently aware that other people were staring at him, but he didn't care.

He felt suddenly, violently moved—he lurched forward as though something had struck him across the shoulders. Doug's father reached out and grasped his shoulder.

"You all right?"

Alden nodded and fought to keep his face neutral. He wanted to smile. He wanted show a grin wrought of both elation and wickedness. He stared at the casket, the still air burning his eyes, and let his heartbeat push blood through his veins to a rapid, thrilling beat.

I didn't kill you, he thought. He had pulled the trigger, yes, but he wasn't the killer. Neither he nor Doug had ever been the cause of death. They had both pulled the trigger, but the responsibility for the ends of those lives rested elsewhere. He remembered what he'd told Tom and Pedro. They had been instruments used by someone else. Alden had intended the words as a convincing lie, but he hadn't been lying at all. They had, indeed, been instruments, but they'd been instruments invisible to the player.

"You sure you're all right?" Doug's father asked.

Alden looked at him and nodded again. "Yeah," he replied, "I'm okay. I just need to get out of here. When's the funeral?"

"Tomorrow at noon."

"Saint Joseph's?"

"Yeah."

"I'll be there," Alden said. "I just have to go."

"It's okay, Al. I understand."

"Yeah, I just need to get some fresh air and think. I haven't been able to get a lot of sleep, you know?"

"It's okay, really. We'll see you tomorrow."

"Who's going to be there?" Alden asked.

"Same people."

"Okay."

Alden turned and walked away from the casket. He passed Tiffany and gave her a strong, heavy look and single, forceful nod. Doug's father didn't understand at all. No one did, but that was okay, because there was a way to bring everything into balance again.

He stopped at the post office near his house before going home. He waited in line for a few minutes before stepping up to the counter where he was greeted by a thin, gray-haired man.

"Can I help you?"

"I have an international package coming," Alden said, "but I'm moving and I was hoping it could be forwarded."

After getting home, Alden slept through the afternoon and the night. He changed his underwear in the morning, but wore the same black shirt and pants. There was no use putting on something new today. He was ready to leave well before the funeral was scheduled to start, but he wasn't planning on attending the service.

Instead, he carried his computer, a rucksack filled with clothes, and a few trash bags to his car. The sky was gray and rain was falling, sometimes softly and sometimes in furious bursts. It was finally the perfect kind of weather for the day. He lingered outside his door for a while, letting the drops wet his hair. The wind was steady and cool, gusting occasionally and making the heavy air sting his skin. He closed his eyes and smiled and let time slip past.

He left after the funeral had started. He drove through the city and into the mistreated suburbs. The cathedral sat next to the cemetery where Mark had been buried. Doug's plot wouldn't be far from his friend's. Alden parked in front of the tall white steeple and waited half an hour for the great wooden doors to open.

Doug's relatives carried the casket. Alden joined the pedestrian procession as they crossed the street and entered the graveyard through the black iron gate. He fell in step with Tiffany and she reached out and took his hand. He held it until they stopped on the wet grass around the fresh hole in the earth.

The rain was steady. It pattered off of dark umbrellas and one black cowboy hat—it belonged to one of Doug's relatives. Alden thought he was from Arkansas or Kentucky, but he wasn't sure. The priest spoke, but Alden didn't pay attention. He spent the time looking back over his shoulder toward Tom's house, so close to the bodies of his friends. It made his blood feel cool enough under his skin that the rain seemed warm.

When the priest had said a final prayer, Alden left. He didn't speak to Doug's parents or Tiffany. He walked across the wet grass and through the black gate and slid behind the wheel. His car was the first to drive away. He drove in silence, the radio off and his mind calm. There was no more thinking to be done. It wasn't about thought and planning anymore. It wasn't even about vengeance.

This was about doing right.

He drove past the construction barriers and the orange barrels slowly, then turned left into the arboreal condominium development. It was darker under the boughs of the old, wide shade trees. The rain fell oddly on the windshield, the drops made heavier and more random by the leaves. He drove around to the right and parked on the street behind a green American sedan with rust around the wheel wells.

He got out of the car. The condos here had old, brown siding and the white paint around the window frames was cracked or chipped. He walked around his car to the sidewalk and continued deeper into the development. He looked at the homes on his right, examining the windows for any motion, but he saw none. The weather was bad. People would probably want to stay inside.

He saw the condo he was looking for ahead. A blue station wagon was parked in the driveway—that was good. He walked past the car and took the two concrete steps up to the door in one stride. He pushed the doorbell with his knuckle and waited. The door opened a moment later. The young woman inside stood still for a moment, looking at him in confusion and pulling at her curly black hair.

"Alden?" she asked.

He nodded and wiped his eyes and said, "Hey, Andrea."

"What's going on?" she asked in a quiet, uneasy voice.

"Did you know Doug's dead?" he asked her.

"Oh my God. No. What happened?"

"He was murdered," Alden said, stepping forward.

She backed up and let him inside. He put the back of his hand on the door and closed it as she moved farther into the living room. She was wearing a gray tank top and pink sweatpants. Music was playing on a stereo in the corner—a woman singing softly. The television was off against the far wall, just beside the archway into a hall. Alden had never been inside before and he looked around appraisingly. The hardwood floor was in good condition and covered by a large, patterned rug of red and brown. The sofa was leather and the television was a large flat panel type. She had nice things, Alden thought.

"I'm so sorry," Andrea said, her hazel eyes now glistening beneath slight furrows over her nose.

"Do you have something to drink?" Alden asked.

"Sure," she said.

He followed her into the hall. The kitchen was on the left. His dress shoes squeaked on the gray linoleum floor as he pivoted and leaned against the counter next to the sink. There were a few dishes waiting to be done. A can opener sat beside a wooden block from which several knives protruded. Alden looked at them as Andrea opened the refrigerator.

"What do you want?" she asked, looking back at him.

"What do you have?"

She turned back to the refrigerator and he reached into his pocket for a pair of latex gloves. He pulled them over his hands. His palms stuck to the rubber slightly, but he was already adjusting the fit between his fingers when she turned around again. She looked at him and her head moved back and to the side. Her lips moved forward and together. "Wha—"

Alden lunged forward. He struck her hard with the heel of his hand and felt her nose break to the side. She screamed and fell back into the door of the refrigerator, clinging to it to stay on her feet. Blood rushed over her lips and fell from her chin. Alden felt his heart leap as his own blood accelerated; his entire body tingled and felt warm and yearned for destructive motion.

He stepped close to her and grabbed a handful of her curly hair. She cried out and tried to kick him, but he turned his hips away and struck her in the face again, cracking her nose crooked. She fell to the floor and he let her drop. It gave him time to return to the wooden block and draw out a boning knife.

She turned over onto her hands and knees and tried to scurry into the hallway. Alden kicked her hard in the side of the head. Her skull struck the side of the refrigerator and she collapsed to the floor. Alden reached down and dragged her by the hair. She was still conscious and she struggled weakly as he pulled her into the living room. He lifted her by the hair and threw her onto the leather couch.

He stood in front of her, feet wide apart and shoulders square. He held the knife casually in his right hand and waited. She was dazed and her head was bleeding from a gash where it had hit the refrigerator. It took a few minutes for her to blink her eyes and move her head slightly side to side. Then she saw the knife and gasped, suddenly shocked into greater mental clarity.

"If you scream," Alden told her, "I'll kill you."

"What are you d-doing?"

He watched her as she ran her hands over her bloody tank top and looked at the red color on her fingers, still too alarmed to feel the pain. He stepped closer and adjusted his grip on the knife.

"Do you know what you've done?" he asked rhetorically.

"Alden, please! What are you doing?"

"Do you know how many people you've killed?"

"I don't know what you're talking about!" she shouted. "I haven't killed anyone! Please, Alden! What's going on? Put down the knife! Please, Alden! Pl—"

He stepped forward and slashed the knife right-to-left, cutting deeply into her left cheek. She squealed and grabbed the wound and fell onto her side on the couch. Alden took her by the hair again and forced her upright, his face nearly touching hers and the edge of the knife at her throat.

"Five," Alden said coolly. "You've killed five people."

Her eyes were wide and wet. She shook her head slightly, a quivering motion, and said, "I haven't ki—"

He stabbed her. He thrust the knife into the side of her gut, just below the left side of her ribcage, then withdrew it. She screamed, but he put his hand over her mouth to muffle the sound. She cried and tried to double over, but he held her in a sitting position with his gloved hand grasping her jaw.

He stared at her bloody face, then shoved her backward into the couch and stepped back. The glove on his left hand was bright red with her blood as he raised his fingers one at a time, counting.

"Mark!" he said. "You killed him by dragging him down into the filthy pit you dug out with needles and spoons."

She pressed her hands against the wound in her side, eyes locked on Alden's bloody hand as he continued. "Tom! You killed him when you opened your legs for his dirty money and what you *thought* was power. Doug pulled the trigger, but *you* made that happen."

Andrea's eyes, then almost shut from pain, went wide.

"Pedro!" Alden went on. "He was dead the moment you starting fucking Tom for free dope, but I had to end that."

Alden stepped forward again and Andrea screamed. He flipped the knife around in his hand, and with the blade down, jammed it hard into her left leg. She wailed and writhed and he twisted the blade, then drew it out and moved away again to continue counting.

"Jennifer!" he shouted. "She was just a mixed up girl, but you killed her, too! She had nothing to do with this, but you put her in the way of all this hurt. You see what you do? You see what you've done? I had to put two bullets in her brain. You forced me to do that to a teenage girl who had nothing to do with this!"

Andrea was quieter. She whimpered and twisted on the couch, curled up to shield her left side from more abuse. Alden watched her and felt his heart slow. He felt the same sense of righteous indignation he'd felt having coffee with Mark's mother. He stepped forward and Andrea cringed, but he didn't touch her. He leaned in close.

"Doug," he whispered. "I had to shoot the only friend I had left in the head. You killed him, my only friend. Do you understand? It all started with you and your pot, your coke, your smack."

"Alden," Andrea pleaded.

"Now it's all come back on you," he told her. "All the suffering you've caused and all the lives you've taken—it's all coming back to you."

"Please."

"Pleased?" Alden asked moving away. "Yes, I am, because I've found what I needed to find. You know, I've done a lot of things. I've sold people useless shit they didn't need for a paycheck. I've delivered food to people who didn't give a damn about me. I've even been a cop, but you know, none of that was right for me."

Andrea, her pink sweatpants now shining with blood, looked at Alden with horrified eyes.

"I suppose," he went on, "I should thank you for that, at least. For all the pain you've caused, for all the death you've caused—the death you forced *me* to deal—I've finally found my way. See, this is it. In this moment, in this one experience, I know I'm doing something good. You've killed five people and caused unknown pain to so many others. Christ, you've destroyed entire families, and today I have the privilege of making sure you don't do any more damage."

"No," Andrea wept, shaking her head. "No, Alden. No."

"I thought I crossed a line," he whispered, "but now I see the world clearly. There are no lines, only ends."

Alden turned the knife around in his hand again. Andrea was still shaking her head when he moved in and started slashing. He swung his arm in uncontrolled arcs, slicing at her as she screamed. She brought her arms up and he cut into them. She curled her legs in front of her body and he cut into them. He continued until she was a shuddering, wincing mass of pain and fear.

He was breathing hard when he stopped and pushed himself from atop her stained flesh and clothes. He watched her quiver for several seconds. He could feel her hot blood on his face and soaking through his clothes. After a long moment he grabbed her by the hair and pulled her from the couch. She had no strength remaining and fell onto the rug with a thump. Alden rolled her onto her stomach. He parted the hair on the back of her head and felt for the soft spot at the base of her skull, then placed the tip of the boning knife there. He moved his left hand over the bottom of the knife's handle and struck downward as he pushed, thrusting the knife deep into the back of her neck. Her body jerked and he wrenched the knife back and forth twice.

Andrea was still, her spinal cord severed from her brain. Alden left the knife protruding from the back of her neck and moved away from the corpse. The couch was covered in streaks of blood. His gloves were slick with it and his clothes were stained, but it was difficult to see on the black material.

The music was still playing, the soft voice quietly lamenting lost love. Alden listened for a few minutes until the song was over. He paused a few seconds more, then went to the door and turned the handle to open it an inch. He removed the gloves and put them in his pocket, then opened the door with his foot and stepped outside. His shoes left bloody footprints on the concrete steps, so he walked on the grass instead of the sidewalk. A car passed by, but the driver didn't look at him. He had trash bags in his rucksack to cover the seat of his car.

"After that," he whispered to himself, "business as usual."

He'd never seen real farmland before. There were farms in Vermont, but they weren't like these. Here, under a sky of fiery orange that smoldered a sultry red near the horizon, the fields stretched as far as he could see on either side of the Interstate. No lakes and no mountains, just fields and sky.

The beautiful, peaceful country was interrupted only by a well-lit line of toll booths ahead. The Interstate widened and he moved into one of the lanes that accepted cash.

"You're getting pretty good at this," he told himself.

There were only a few cars ahead of him. He reached over to the black duffel bag on the passenger seat. He'd stashed a handful of coins in one of the side pockets and he took out the correct amount as he pulled up to the booth. He dropped the money into the half-cone receptacle and the red light ahead of him turned green. The middle-aged man in the booth smiled and waved. He returned the gesture and accelerated.

The sun was low and the blazing orange sky was gradually falling into the sanguine horizon. He drove on, a smirk playing across his lips as he took the easy curves of the road. He scratched at his neck—the hair there was caught somewhere in the itchy limbo between stubble and beard, but that would pass.

He saw a sign up ahead. It wasn't green or yellow and it was large. He squinted in the lengthening shadows until his headlights swept over the sign's width. It was bright blue with a red outline of the state in the middle. It welcomed him, declaring that he had reached the "Crossroads of America."

He smiled and drove on, speeding west into the red sky. His chest felt tight and he blinked his eyes clear as tears started to gather. Somewhere ahead, in some sprawling city or some small town, someone needed what he had to offer. He was sure of that. For the first time, his existence mattered. He would make a difference.

Somewhere ahead, he would make something right again.